SONGBIRD IN THE DARKEST NIGHT

A SONGS OF THE NIGHT NOVELLA

D. KATHLEEN McATEER

SONGBIRD IN THE DARKEST NIGHT

First edition. August 2025
ISBN 978-1-950879-79-3 (paperback)
Wednesday Ink, LLC

If you would like permission to use material from the book (other than review purposes) please contact the author directly at mcateerdk@gmail.com. Thank you for your support of authors rights!

Website: dkathleenmcateer.com

THE SONGBIRD'S MUSIC

To my best friend, who just so happened to become my eternal lover. I will hold your hand even in the darkest night.

AUTHOR'S NOTE

Songbird in the Darkest Night is a novella set eighty-three years before *Daughter of the Dark Sun*. This work is best read after Volume One, and before Volume Two.

This is a **dark romance** as well as a **dark fantasy**. Please read all the content and trigger warnings before reading this story.

Depictions of adult themes such as: psychological manipulation, allusions to sexual assault between the FMC and a side character (in the past), attempted murder, ritualistic self-harm, alcohol abuse, voyeurism, and open door scenes with a virgin MMC that include blood play and BDSM dynamics.

PLAYLISTS

IN THE WORLD OF Eás, music is power. Below are two short playlists for Renata and Aeslev; each song corresponds to their respective chapters in chronological order.

Scan below and enjoy!

RENATA

AESLEV

I know why the Songbird sings.
She sings for love despite the fear,
despite the darkness of the night.

My Songbird is a wild thing.
But love need not be a cage, my dear.
I will hold you, yet not too tight.

I only wish to set you free.

One

BLOOD & SALT

RENATA

ONCE FOR THE BETRAYER.

Renata sucked in a breath through clenched teeth, then pulled downward with her right hand. Her long, dark brown fingers trembled, but she did not let go of the jeweled hilt. A wave of pain assaulted her left hand as the black blade sliced across her palm. Hot, bright red blood rushed forth, spilling from her broken skin into the sea foam gathering at her feet. With a hiss, Renata grabbed the hilt with her left hand, sticky blood smearing across sparkling blue gems set in a gleaming silver hilt. She winced as they dug into her palm, tearing at the wound.

Once for the Kinslayer!

A shiver raced down the young woman's spine as she walked further into the sea. The cold waves lapped at her calves. Something slithered between her legs; Renata clutched the dagger tightly and waded forth until the water reached her hips. Shivers wracked her body accustomed to the relentless heat of the sun. The Shadow-weave curled around her did little to lessen the stinging cold of the black sea.

Once for the Betrayer. Once for the Kinslayer!

Renata held her arms out and placed the dagger—the metal somehow colder than even the icy sea itself—to her right palm. With a scream that sounded more like a thousand dying souls than a singular woman, she dragged the blade over her tender flesh. Searing pain raced across her hand and through her arm, a shockwave that only gathered strength as it pierced her mind.

A soft woman's voice mingled with the dizzying waves of pain, but her words could not break through.

No, come back to me! I will find you, I will, I will!

As the pain eased, Renata looked to the east, her gaze settled on the sunrise. Soft oranges and muted pinks colored the far horizon, an endless stretch of black water between her and the sun she yearned to feel. Her lips quivered for but a moment before she straightened her back, pushing away thoughts of who she left in the desert oasis she called home.

"Take it, take my blood, you thieving bitch!" She clenched her hands until the crimson liquid dripped from each closed fist. "Taste what you failed to erase!"

Renata closed her eyes, standing in the black seas with blood dripping from both hands, a dagger in one, until her heart knew nothing but rage. It grew until a song burst to life inside her mind. It bent her every thought, intertwined with the muscles around her bones, poured into her veins, filling her with a desire stronger than even love itself.

Revenge.

She opened her eyes, now black as the night sky when the moon dies, a bitter laugh growing in her throat.

"One day, the world will learn of your crimes! She will walk Eás again, and you will tremble to behold Her wrath! I vow this, with my blood, with my shadows, with my future children. Run, run, run if you are wise!"

Renata stood in the black sea, waves assaulting her thin frame, until the tears poured from her soul. Her eyes stung with each bitter droplet spilled, but she did not try to hold them back. It was the only thing Renata could do: curse the Betrayer, spill her blood into the angry sea, and let the tears pull the ache from her heart.

Soon, the pain would end. Her Goddess would walk Eás again, and the Shadow-weave would not be tainted with her dying screams. One day, the hole in her heart would disappear, and Renata would finally know peace. But until then, the only thing she could do was cry.

"GODS, WHAT AM I going to tell Aes this time?" Renata muttered to herself while securing the final bandage around her right hand. She winced as a bolt of pain raced through her arm. "Maybe I can find a Greenweaver before he sees. It could heal, could be just another crease in my palm."

Not wanting to think about Aeslev, her closest friend since childhood, the young woman turned her attention to packing her campsite. Situated on a low cliff overlooking the raging black sea, it was her favorite of the three sites her father showed her years before. The small copse of acacia and palm trees along the cliff edge offered her more protection than anywhere else. But, more importantly, it was a reminder of home. She couldn't help but smile anytime her clothes caught on the thorny limbs of the acacias, memories of Aeslev's many unfortunate encounters with the ferocious predators always floating by.

Be wary, Reni. The Blue Ships have not been seen for years, but my heart warns me against them. Stay low, stay out of sight, and never light a fire, no matter how cold you get. Remember what your mother taught you, but use the Sunweave only if necessary. You were lucky before, my sweet. I shudder to think what may happen if the Shadows grow angry when you are alone.

Her father's words rang out like an alarm in her mind. Renata dropped to the ground and pressed her cheek to the rough stone below, nearly the same cool brown as her skin. Silent. *Well, at least it isn't sandraiders.* With a groan, she shimmied her way to the cliff edge. A gasp escaped her lips at the sight.

A dozen massive white ships with bright blue sails floated across the black sea where, not even an hour ago, she had spilled her blood in an accursed family ritual. Renata shut her eyes, overcome by fear that somehow, someway, the people on board would sniff her out and expose the maiden's secrets. Gulping down the cool, salty air, she crawled back to the bag she unceremoniously dropped a moment before.

Shit, I need to get out of here. Why the fuck are the Reavers here? Fuck fuck fuck!

For nearly fifty years, the once oft-sighted Blue Ships from the East had all but disappeared from the southern coast of the Madhira Desert. *Reavers*, the locals called them. Blood-thirsty pirates who stopped any ship, no matter how insignificant, and demanded a ransom for safe passage from Gisamir to the eastern port city of Twins' Port. Yet, one day they disappeared, sailing into the West, never to be seen again. The locals celebrated their departure, certain they had finally left after hundreds of years spent terrorizing the coast.

Yet, time proved them wrong, and one day, the raids began again. A hard-faced woman with cobalt blue hair who declared herself *The Mother* demanded that all pay homage to Aslyren. Any who dared enter the black seas found themselves at the mercy of strange people with pale skin and blue hair, eyes as cold as the endless waters they claimed dominion over. The *Asliri*, they called themselves, followers of the Maiden of the East, the goddess Aslyren herself. To the Madhiri, they were a nuisance best ignored by staying out of the sea. An unspoken commandment all were willing to follow; all, except Renata and her family.

Though she did not fear the Asliri—indeed, some days she wished to test her Shadows against the interlopers—Renata never intended to let her presence be known to them. *Beware the Easterlings, for House Anatnará will surely perish if they learn of us.* Something all born into her family knew, ingrained in them before they could even utter a word. She could not shake the feeling that the Blue Ships below searched for something—or someone—in the desert.

Renata stooped low and shoved what little belongings she had left to pack into the satchel. With one final glance around to ensure her presence did not linger, she took off for the tree line. Her task now completed—though with little time to spare—she turned her mind away from the Reavers below.

One day, justice would find them. One day, but not today. Today, Renata could only think of returning home at long last and all the dozens of sketches she wanted to show Aeslev.

Two

GOLDEN PROMISES

AESLEV

"**W**ELL, ARE YOU GOING to stand there gawking all day? Come, Aeslev, meet your bride-to-be."

The words of his father barely cut through the daze. *Bride-to-be.* Traded off like a bargaining chip with no regard to his wishes and used to chase his mother's aspirations.

"It is a shame the Lady Nessaeren has a *liraes* after all," his father continued, "but her sister is the second-born and still holds a great deal of power."

"Oh, my son!" cried out his mother, a smile cracking her forever placid face. "She is a beauty, but of course, all the women from House Isht'iri are. One of the Named Houses, and a Daughter of the Sun at that! Soon you'll have children, and House Caledir will be forever remembered as one of the strongest of the Weavers."

His mother, a woman with somber brown eyes and clay-red hair, rushed forward and threw her arms around the man, who stood still like a statue. He wanted to push her away, to scream at her to stop living his life for him for once. Instead, Aeslev blinked away the tears growing in his eyes—one dark brown, the other a deep green—and put a hand on his mother's shoulder.

"Yes, Mama," he ground out, each word a dagger to his heart. "It is a great honor for our House indeed."

Aeslev winced as thoughts of Renata, his childhood friend for as long as he could remember, pushed through. Her glittering smile when he made a gods-awful pun. How her eyes shifted from dark gray to silver at night, and oh, gods, that last hug she gave him, squeezing him like he was the only thing that mattered in the world. For nearly twenty-two years she was just a friend, just another Weaver who would break their back for their masters. But now, he dreamed of her being more.

I wish you didn't have to leave. The Southern Edge is dangerous, and the sandraiders are growing bolder by the year.

You wouldn't understand, Aes. I have to go, I have to do this. It's... it's nothing. Don't worry about me, please. I'll be fine, I've done this before with Papa.

You're only getting more stubborn with age, Ren.

And you're only getting to be more of a pain in my ass, Aes.

Do you want me to stop?

Never, you silly boy.

Ren...

Why couldn't he have finished that sentence? Why did he have to choke on his words, to let the woman leave for dangerous lands, gone for weeks on end for some secret errand that even her best friend could not know? Now he stood with his parents on the white marble floors of the Temple, a veiled woman—no, his future *wife*—waiting for him a few paces away.

"Excuse me," he said before pushing his mother away.

Aeslev swallowed, forcing the spit past the rising lump in his throat, and walked to the strange woman arrayed in yellows and reds. Her warm, ocher skin seemed to glow as she stepped into a shaft of sunlight. Bright azure blue flaming suns and flying doves adorned her hands and forearms, the tattoos a marking of her nobility.

House Isht'iri, The House of the Flame-Blessed. One of the four Houses of the Sun, all flowing with the divine blood of the Sun Goddess, Myrniar. The women of House Isht'iri were said to be almost as beautiful as the lost Goddess herself. Not that any of that mattered to Aeslev. A pretty face, perfect skin, tight coils of black and scarlet hair—nothing could compare to the woman who already owned his heart.

Renata, with her soft auburn hair that fell in gentle waves to her waist, the silken locks so different from the textured hair of the rest of the Madhiri. Her gray eyes that glimmered silver at night, dancing as if the stars themselves lit up her soul. Her crooked smile, a dimple forming under the left edge of those full lips that always said his name with such care. Her skin, always slightly cool to the touch, and how her fingers often lingered just a moment too long.

But she could never be more, even if Aeslev controlled his destiny. Renata made it clear long ago; she prized her freedom above all else. How could he be so selfish and shackle her to a life with him?

With a grimace, Aeslev turned his thoughts to the woman waiting under a bouquet of lilies. A gentle wind blew past, carrying with it the soft scent of the woman intermingled with the flowers. He bent down on one knee and lowered his head to her outstretched hand. Delicate golden bangles encrusted with rubies and white gemstones slid down her wrist, the musical sound filling the room. Her hand was soft and hot to the touch, as if the sun itself burnt within her heart.

"*Héna'sera*, Lady Naraniél. You honor me greatly to let me clasp your hand, Daughter of the Sun."

The woman, face still hidden behind a pale golden veil, touched Aeslev's cheek and traced a swirling pattern with her fingers. Sparks of energy crackled across his skin under her touch until he thought he might burst into flames. Then, before it became too much to bear, her hand fell away, and with it, the strand of Sunweave she wove into his soulsong. Aeslev shuddered; never had he felt such raw power before.

"*Kïra ùsh seren glaich,*" the veiled woman said with a soft voice, like water gently flowing through a stream. "*Mi che itu' dlaych maï feilira.*"

The woman spoke in the Elder Tongue, words only those in the Houses of the Sun and a few privileged Named Houses knew. It dawned on Aeslev just how different this woman was from everything he knew. How could they ever find common ground, a Lady from behind the Wall and a Weaver who worked the fields? Even if his heart did not belong to another, he never pictured himself with blue tattoos on his hands and a woman of unearthly beauty in his bed. He could not say why, but something about the Named Houses and their worship of the lost Sun Goddess set his heart on edge.

"Come, rise, *maí feilira.*"

As Aeslev stood, Lady Naraniél flipped back the shimmering golden veil. He looked up to see a round face with a bright smile and emerald green eyes studying him. Her beauty rivaled that of her elder sister, the High Lady Nessaeren. Aeslev's promised bride, mere months before, until one day she declared her undying love for another Weaver, calling him her fated lover, her *liraes.* Aeslev felt a weight lift from his chest that day, and naively thought himself freed from his mother's scheming.

Now, he looked into the bright green eyes of a woman equally as beautiful—and equally as unwanted.

"Soon we will be married, according to the wishes of the *Makhaeren.* It is a great honor for both our families to have the strongest Skyweaver from House Caledir join my House of the Sun. It is a shame my sister will not have such a handsome man by her side," she said with a smile. Whether she meant it or not mattered little to Aeslev. He would marry her out of duty, give her children, and then find whatever he could to forget about Renata.

"You flatter me, my Lady, to say I could be even half as comely as the men from behind the Wall." Aeslev paused, grinding his teeth together until his jaw ached. He sucked in a breath of air, then uttered a sentence he vowed to never say to anyone but Renata. "I am yours, my lady, and I humbly accept your soulbond."

Lady Naraniél replied, but the words floated past Aeslev.

Ren, Ren, oh gods, Ren.

His heart hammered within his chest, an ache forming until he thought it might explode.

Why did you have to leave? Why couldn't I just finish that sentence? Where are you, why, why, why?

He gulped down the arid desert air, but it did little to calm the raging storm inside.

This isn't right, but I don't know what else to do. I love you, but is this how I am to do it? Married to another, forced to never see you again?

Aeslev smiled through the pain, doing the only thing he could: survive.

Three

DOOMED LOVE

COME BACK TO ME, *Mireithren.*

Renata's eyes flew open at the strange name that seemed somehow so familiar. She had just enough time to lean over the side of her bed before spilling the contents of her queasy stomach over the hard dirt floor. Her vision swam as the room slowly came into focus. Four red clay walls. A basin with water, the wood faded with age. A small piece of polished silver on the wall above it, reflecting what meager light made its way through the curtains.

With a groan, Renata rolled to her other side. The cool winter air eased the heat racing across her skin, a wildfire that started in her belly and spread with each beat of her heart. She tried to find her breath; it took a moment, but soon she was inhaling on the count of three, exhaling on the count of four. *In, in, in. Out, out, out, out. In, in, in. Out, out, out, out.* She kept breathing like this for some time until a chill settled over her skin. She pulled the cotton covers close, then closed her eyes again.

But sleep would not return to the woman. She kept whispering the name *Mireithren* to herself, trying to understand why she knew it. Someone she met, perhaps? A relative mentioned in stories, long since dead? A maiden from the Named Houses? No, no, and a resounding no.

Mireithren.

"It cannot be Her," Renata whispered, yet even as she denied the thought, her heart lurched at the possibility. Could it be, could the end be near? Finally, after thousands of years of cursed shadows and hidden secrets, would the world learn the truth?

"Reni!"

Renata did not reply, too consumed by thoughts of the mysterious dream. A man with curly black hair like Aeslev's and silvery-gray eyes held a woman close, one cheek marred by criss-crossing black scars. Her eyes shone bright amber in a face so ethereal it could only belong to a Goddess. The Goddess? *Her* Goddess?

"Renata!"

Coils of black hair, glinting with gold, fell to the divine woman's waist. Warmth seemed to radiate from her; everything about the woman was so full of life.

"RENATA!"

A loud knock on the door startled Renata out of her thoughts. She leapt up, stumbling over her feet before crashing into the small dresser near the bed.

"I'm fine!" she shouted before the man on the other side could react. "Just a minute, Papa!"

Renata stood, then quickly pulled a thin black dress over her head. She glanced in the polished silver that passed as a mirror, smoothing her wild waves before throwing the door open.

"Papa!" she exclaimed as she threw her arms around the man just outside her bedroom door. "Papa, I did it! It took me longer than I... Papa, what is wrong?"

Nazith, Renata's father, stood with a solemn face, eyes thick with tears. He pulled his daughter in close, clasping one hand around the back of her head and the other around her shoulders. The taste of bile crept into Renata's mouth.

"Papa?" she asked, her voice barely more than a whisper.

"Reni, oh gods, Reni, I am so sorry."

No, no, no, no, no, it's not that. It's not that, it's not that, it's not that.

"Renata, *myrserin.*" Nazith paused for a moment and showered her head with kisses. It did little to ease her broken heart. "I tried. But her sister chose him, and his parents would never reject such a match."

A keening sound split the air, a cry from the depths of her soul echoing emotions that Renata had kept hidden even from herself. She began to shake in her father's wiry, russet-brown arms. He pulled her closer, his breath warm against her neck.

"Then I will never see him again?" she asked with a trembling voice.

"It is still a week away, *myrserin*."

"A week?" The blood pounded in her ears, a force so vicious she thought it might split her skull. "I only have a week to say my goodbyes? To fill a lifetime of memories with my closest friend? That is not enough! They can't take him away like this!"

As grief and hatred for the Named Houses twisted around her heart, the Song of the Night roared to life. Shadows swirled around her feet, rising behind Renata like an angry army ready to burst forth and raze the desert. A chill settled over her, seeping deep into her bones until she could barely remember what the sun felt like against her skin. A woman's scream tore through her brain like a hot knife. It seared her mind until overwhelming grief drowned out all else.

"Reni, shhh. Come back to me, *myrserin*."

Her father's words cut through the baleful hatred of the Shadow-weave. Renata opened her eyes and sucked in a breath through clenched teeth. The shadows dimmed, then faded altogether.

"He can still say no, Reni."

"He won't!" she cried out. "Aeslev would never hurt his parents like that. He is a good man, Papa. He would never choose me."

"But do you want him to? I know how happy you were when Nessaeren announced she found a *liraes*."

Renata pushed her father away, turning quickly before he could see the silent tears spilling from her eyes. Of course she loved Aeslev; hadn't she always, in truth? But he loved his parents more, always doing his best to make his House proud. It was the burden of the Skyweavers, always putting their House ahead of love. How could Aeslev be any different? Renata told herself long ago that the most selfish thing she could do in life was admit how she felt for the man destined for greatness. But now that the time came, the reality of what it meant hurt more than she realized.

"I don't want to lose him forever, Papa. But... but... I can't. I can't cast my shadow over his future."

"Reni, oh my sweet Reni. Come here, my girl." Nazith caught her wrist in his hand. He pulled her close, turning her head to wipe the tears away. "Do you hear yourself? What would your mother say if she were still here?"

"You deserve love, because love made you." She recited the words almost automatically, a mantra her mother said relentlessly in her youth. "Oh, Papa, but how could Mama understand? You are both shadewalkers, it was never a question of love or doom!"

"Doom? Doom, Renata?" Nazith tightened his grip on her wrist. "Don't you ever speak such words about the Shadow-weave or Our Lady ever again." A fire blazed in his eyes she had never seen before; she tried to pull away, but shadows rooted her in place.

"Papa?" she squeaked out.

"I cannot force you to accept love, but I will never tolerate such rot from your mouth. You know the history of the Disco—"

"Oh, Papa, please! I am sorry, please! Don't lecture me right now, I beg of you."

Nazith let her go, evidently satisfied with her plea. Renata shrank away from her father, stunned by the ferocity she witnessed. *Gods, am I really being that stupid? I've never seen Papa so angry before.*

"I need some air, Papa. I'll be home for dinner."

Before he could reply, Renata rushed past him, flying out the door and onto the sands warmed by the midday sun. Despite the warmth around her, a coldness grew in her heart. She wished she could run away from these feelings, run away and come back to find out it was all a cruel joke.

I love you, Aes. Can you ever love me?

Four

BLISS IN THE DARK

"**W**HY ARE YOU STARING *at me like that? Come and finish the job, silly boy.*"

"*A boy can't do this.*"

A moan fills the air as lips find the crease of an inner thigh. Teeth graze against the soft skin, and the scent of vanilla mixed with sweat fills the air.

"*A boy plays games, like—*"

A nip at the tender flesh cuts off the taunting words. A hand strays upwards, skimming the surface of flesh ready to burst into flames.

"*Gods, you smell so fucking good. My favorite meal of the day. Mine to devour... And devour I shall.*"

Lips trail to the side, drawn in by the puckered flesh waiting for release. A tongue flicks across the tender nub, pulling a scream from the woman. A hand pulls the writhing form closer.

"Yes, yes, that's my girl. Scream for me, sweet Songbird."

The first thing to cross Aeslev's mind was how hard his cock was throbbing. The second thought was slower to come. *Why am I dreaming about fucking Ren?* The next thought followed in quick succession. *Ren, oh gods, Ren, I need you.*

Though he'd never once thought of his closest friend when the urges came, tonight Aeslev couldn't get her off his mind. His hand shook above his cock, begging for more. *I don't want to taint her like this. No, gods, pull yourself together, Aes!*

Lightning streaked across his flesh before fading away. One of the most powerful Skyweavers the Madhira had seen in generations, Aeslev's powers often ran wild when overcome with emotion. He learned to control it with time, but something about the woman with cool brown, almost purple skin, and soft gray eyes undid everything in seconds. Maybe it was why he loved her so much; only Renata made him feel truly alive.

With a groan, Aeslev pushed himself from bed. The cool dirt beneath his feet did little to ease the fires inside. He padded to the simple set of drawers at the end of his bed and pulled on a pair of pants, grimacing as his hand brushed against his cock. *Leave it, fucking leave it!*

Aeslev couldn't be sure of the time, but the quiet darkness outside told him it must've been past midnight. He slipped by his parents' door, making sure to avoid the beads his mother had hung the other day in celebration of his engagement. A shiver passed over him as he ducked beneath them.

Soon enough, he made it to the front door, quietly opening and shutting it. The cold winter air helped pull the confused feelings from his heart. With a sigh, Aeslev began walking with no destination in mind.

Married. Soon, he would be married, and a strange woman with divine blood would expect him to fuck her. Give her children, ensure the continuation of her line, and, if she wanted, use him for her pleasure. The thought nauseated him.

Before he could descend into a bitter rage at his future, Aeslev stumbled headfirst into a palm tree. *Shit! Where the hell am I?* He blinked away the pain and looked around. Trees surrounded him; just past a line of palms in front of him stretched Lake Anataerl, glistening in the silvery moonlight. He pushed forward, urged on by the promise of cold water to soothe his aching heart.

As Aeslev cleared the last of the trees, he saw a woman with auburn hair and brown skin that almost seemed to shimmer in the moonlight bathing in the lake. He knew he should turn and leave the naked maiden in peace, but the soft curves of her body called to him. Aeslev watched as she splashed water over her shoulders; the way her muscles moved in the dim moonlight enchanted him. He'd never seen a naked woman before outside of passing glances when the Temple Prostitutes, sacred women the men of the Houses of the Sun used to continue their lines, walked through the streets to celebrate being chosen.

Before he knew what he was doing, a hand slipped past the waistband of his loose pants. Aeslev wrapped it around his cock and began stroking. Every cell in his body screamed for release, begged to quench the fires consuming him from the inside out.

Any sense of shame the man may have felt burnt away, leaving him enraptured by the maiden illuminated by the silver moon.

The woman in the lake turned to the side, but her face remained hidden from view. Her hands strayed across her body, cupping her breasts and clawing at the flesh between her thighs. Was she... was she *pleasuring* herself?

The more her hands moved, the faster Aeslev stroked. Each stroke brought a burst of pleasure, starting from the head of his cock until it pierced his brain. He moved faster, then slower, chasing the feeling that always ended with bliss shattering across his mind. He imagined what it would be like to feel the woman's hand in place of his, her lips on his neck, her legs over his. Was her skin soft? Would she moan as he ran his hands over her breasts?

Aeslev closed his eyes, imagining Renata instead of the woman in the lake. Her sparkling eyes, silver and gray, as her mouth took his cock, stretching those pretty lips that he desperately wished to kiss. Her hands grabbing his thighs, pulling him closer, his hands tracing the curve of her shoulders.

Each stroke brought Aeslev closer to the edge, the release from this burning need just beyond reach.

Flashes of the dream mixed in; his mouth pressed against Renata's soft inner thigh, and oh, gods, the smell of vanilla that always seemed to follow her.

"Oh, oh sweet Songbird! I... *shit*!"

Aeslev sagged back against a tree as he came, the image of Renata in his arms with her lips against his, intertwining with the bliss consuming his body.

He trembled as the reverie faded and the reality of his actions set in. He wiped the cum from his hand on a large palm leaf next to him and pulled his pants up. With a shaky breath, he stood, trying to focus on the air in his lungs.

"Shit, Ren," he choked out. "I swore I'd never dream of you like that. Fuck, fuck, I am th—"

A splash in front of him jerked Aeslev's attention to the water. *The woman!* How could he have forgotten he used two innocent women for his pleasure? Aeslev gulped, then focused his eyes on the lake.

"Renata?" he blurted out.

As he spoke, a gentle roll of thunder echoed above him, drowning out his cry of surprise. For once, he was glad she made him lose control of his powers.

Indeed, under the silvery moonlight, pleasuring herself to whatever dreams she conjured, stood Renata thigh-deep in the blue lake. She faced Aeslev now, eyes closed as one hand pinched a nipple while the other gripped her ass. Wisps of black seemed to curl around her body, almost forming into the shape of a man's hand, pulling at her thighs.

No, not black. Shadows... she... she...

Aeslev couldn't finish untangling his thoughts before Renata's whimper crossed the water to his ears.

"Aes, gods, I wish I could have you."

The shame he felt moments before melted away as the words of his friend since before memory burnt across his mind. *I wish I could have you.* She wanted him, yearned for him, thought of him just as he thought of her. Aeslev's heart thundered in his chest; could he really be so lucky and have a life with Renata forever in his arms?

Gulping down the cool night air, Aeslev crept further into the trees. His thoughts swirled over the words he heard, how dark shadows curled around Renata's naked form, her body even more beautiful than he dreamed of. A part of him wanted to rush forward then and there, declare his undying love for the woman, and abandon the life his mother arranged without his consent. But that would mean exposing himself, admitting that he watched her in this private moment when she thought herself alone. What if she recoiled from him, called him a disgusting creature for intruding?

Unable to bear the thought of Renata's rejection, Aeslev kept walking through the trees, making for the bright patchwork color tents of the Market. He could never let her know about this night. It would be his secret, his one indulgence before he married Naraniél and became a stranger to the woman who owned his heart.

This is for the best. She would have said something if she truly wanted my love.

OBSESSION

A SHIVER RAN DOWN Renata's spine every time Aeslev's eyes wandered to her corner of the Temple. She had been successful so far in avoiding eye contact, but knew her luck would not last as long as his engagement celebration would. She gulped down the last of her spiced mead, letting the taste of nutmeg and cloves take her back to last night.

What's a pretty thing like you doing drowning themself in a goblet of mead?

Why does anyone drink the pain away?

Ah. A scorned lover. You have my sympathies.

Less scorned, more... traded away.

Intriguing. Will another bottle of mead loosen your tongue?

Either that or it'll kill me. Might as well see.

Another!

'Nother, burkeep.

Shure eewyll be fiiiine, s'all gad.

One minute, she had been nursing a goblet of mead; the next, she had wandered into the lake, naked under the last rays of moonlight before the new year began. Maybe it was the oblivion she drank herself into, or perhaps it was years of emotions refusing to stay contained. The only thing Renata remembered was fantasizing about Aeslev's mouth between her thighs as his hands sent sparks of lightning across her skin.

Then, just when the pleasure became undeniable, she saw the man of her dreams creeping through the palms. Drunk off mead and the waves of ecstasy crashing over her, Renata could only continue chasing her climax while Aeslev watched from the shadows. Then he groaned her name, and the only thing keeping her from running out of the water and claiming him right there were the shadows at her feet. The thought of his cock in his hands, eyes trained on her...

"Shit!"

Renata's cry quieted the room as all eyes turned toward her. She stood over a broken pot, a golden liquid pouring from the remnants over the white marble floor. She scrambled to the side and smoothed her dress before looking up.

"The *Makhaeren* must've put out the strong mead tonight!" she exclaimed while plastering a smile on her face and desperately hoping it looked real.

The party-goers turned away and resumed their conversations, leaving Renata to bear her shame alone. She grabbed another goblet from a servant's tray as they walked by, then pressed herself against the cool stone wall as if trying to melt into it.

"I guess it's true what they say, only the weak can't handle their mead."

A man dressed in bright vermilion robes sidled up to Renata, gold and blue flashing as his hands moved in her peripheral. Renata choked on the spit in her mouth. *Why the fuck is he here?*

"Go away, Émerin, before I make you," she growled, averting her eyes from the intruder.

"Oh, I'd love to see you try. Come on, Renna, it's just like old times. You and me, alone in the corner as my hand—"

"Do you tell your wife these stories?" Renata kept her head down, eyes trained on the amber liquid in her gold cup.

"I save them for myself, Sweet Renna," the man crooned, words dripping in her ear like a poison. *Sweet Renna*, as if he could still possibly feel anything for her after their past. "Don't tell me you don't dream of my lips against your thighs at night."

"That night was a fucking mistake. You are a mistake," she hissed through clenched teeth.

A sharp pain, like a hot poker plunging through her stomach, pulled a gasp from Renata. She looked up to see her tormenter's eyes glowing a pale amber as sparks of light raced down his arms. Dozens of freshly tattooed bright blue doves flew across his hands, almost alive as the Sunweave coursed through him. Émerin smiled as she fell into his gaze, just as cruel as the day he took her virginity. Then, the pain vanished from her body. Renata turned to walk away, but his hands—still blazing like the sun—wrapped around her wrist and pulled her close.

"It must kill you, Renna, knowing you rejected a man greater than you'll ever be." He leaned in closer until his breath tickled her neck. "You could have had it all. Been my concubine while Nessaeren slept in my bed. You could be wearing silks right now and be such a pretty little thing for me."

"You are a vile man," she spat back.

Renata wanted to scream, but that meant drawing unwanted attention. Aeslev's attention. Renata didn't know what to say after last night. Should she pretend nothing happened? Surely, if he wanted to be more than a voyeur in the dark, he would have said something by now.

"Go ahead, cry for help. I'm sure everyone else will believe a wretch with tainted blood over the newest High Lord of House Isht'iri."

Renata froze at his words, *tainted blood*. The Shadow-weave lurched inside, sending a sickening wave of fear coursing through her veins. She squeezed her eyes closed, terrified the shadows would give her away. Émerin couldn't possibly know about her family... could he?

"You already took my maidenhead, what more do you need?" she pleaded, voice cracking as she struggled to control her anger. "Let me go, Émerin!"

He only said those things because we were both lonely and the worst of the Weavers. He can't know anything!

"Why? So you can rush to Aeslev and cry for his protection? He won't be around to save you for much longer. You'll see what happens to sniveling bitches who don't understand their place soon enough, Sweet Renna."

The blood pounded in her ears as the Shadow-weave tried to tear free from its cage. Renata always lost command of her shadows around the man who grew up two houses down from hers. A sickly boy born to a strange family, all dismissed the man until his fourteenth nameday, when he woke up with what would be the first of many dreams foretelling the future of the Named Houses.

The man with eyes that sometimes looked black as night tormented Renata for years, trying to force his friendship and claiming that the two of them understood each other more than the rest of the world could know. Then, after a night of far too much mead (at least, that is what Renata told herself), the two wandered off into the Temple Gardens and emerged as lovers—one more reluctant than the other.

"I had every right to end our engagement," she said at last.

"But then you never went off and married. Tell me, did you at least fuck him, Renna? Let him taste how I claimed you first?"

"Maybe I fucked the whole Weavers District after you left, Émerin."

"Oh, *Sweet Renna*," Émerin's grip tightened around her wrist. "If a weak Sunweaver goes missing and House Isht'iri gets a new servant, no one will care. Oh, maybe the man you love will care for a minute, but then he'll have a wife of his own to fuck and you'll fade to nothing."

"Émerin, don't!" Renata tried to sound commanding, but the words stuck in her throat.

"I'll fuck you again if you ask nicely, Renna."

"Blue is decidedly not your color, *shain're.*"

Renata's head whipped around as Aeslev's voice cut through the cruel words of her captor. Émerin dropped her wrist, smoothing his orange robes before plastering a wide smile on his deep mahogany face.

"Move," Aeslev commanded. "Now."

Émerin kept his eyes trained on Renata. He opened his mouth as if to say something, but before he could utter a sound, a bolt of lightning struck the ground next to his feet.

"I said fucking MOVE!" Aeslev shouted. The music stopped instantly, and all eyes turned to the dark corner where Renata cowered behind Aeslev.

"I am the High L–"

"I don't care if you're the reincarnation of Myrniar herself. You don't belong here, Émerin, and you certainly don't belong anywhere near Renata. She made it clear years ago that you are no longer welcome in her life."

A woman dressed in pale green silks scurried up and whispered something to Émerin. His face paled; as if carried by a gust of wind, he flew out of the room after the woman. A murmur worked through the crowd, and soon all eyes were turned away from the woman fighting with all her might to contain the shadows in her soul.

"Ren, gods, did he hurt you?" Aeslev turned to face Renata, a grimace on his face as he stroked her arm. She recoiled, unable to trust that his touch would not unleash the darkness inside.

"It's nothing. Pay me no mind, this is your engagement party!" She desperately wanted to pretend nothing was wrong. *Please go away, Aes.* "It is a great honor for you, my lord."

Renata pushed against Aeslev and darted out from under his arm, making for the nearest exit from the grand courtyard. Aeslev protested, but his words were lost amidst the din of conversation and music. Renata quickened her pace, then broke into a run once she could no longer hear the music. She kept running over the smooth marble floors of the Temple until she found herself in a small courtyard with no way out.

I need to get away from this wretched desert!

Six

A THING OF BEAUTY

"RENATA, WAIT!"

Aeslev's plea hung in the air, engulfing Renata with the heart-wrenching sense of urgency behind those two simple words.

Ren, wait.

Ren, not Renata. Ren, not Weaver. Ren, not "person who is about to be below my rank".

Guilt tore at her heart, slicing the tender thing until she could hear its dying scream echoing in her mind. *It is a great honor for you, my lord. My lord,* as if he had already bound his soul with the divine woman, as if he were already untouchable. She couldn't look up, couldn't see the pain cracking across the eyes of the man she loved.

"We should not be together," she whispered, focusing on a crack in the garden path beneath her feet. "You are promised to wed the Lady Naraniél, and soon the sands will be unclean for your blessed feet. Forget about me, I am nothing."

"I am so fucking tired of everyone living my life for me," Aeslev growled, an edge to his voice Ren had never heard before. "Renata, look at me."

Before she could comply—or, more likely, continue staring at the crack that echoed her broken heart—Aeslev's hand wrapped around her chin, wrenching her gaze up to his. His one dark eye now looked black as the moonless night, while his green eye swirled with rivulets of gold. A slight storm built at his fingertips, the sound of rolling thunder disturbing the quiet courtyard.

"Please tell me what happened back there. Did... did I say something?"

His eyes studied her face; Renata felt stripped naked under his sweeping gaze, her emotions, which she always hid so easily, now read with ease. Renata let out a deep sigh, letting the cool winter air push back the heat rising in her chest. *I won't taint him, I won't, I won't! Gods, why are you doing this, Aes? Why can't you just let me go?*

"I'm no good for you, Aes," she murmured at last, trying to wrench her gaze away from his. His grip tightened around her chin as his thumb slid up and caressed the fullness of her lower lip. A burst of sunfire spread from where his thumb rested against her skin; it took every bit of her resolve not to melt right there and lean into his embrace.

"Please let me go," she said instead, trying to cool the fires growing inside.

"Only when you tell me what happened."

"I..." The words turned to ash on Renata's tongue. How could he ever understand?

"Did that privileged little shit tell you you're no good?" His eyes darkened, a shadow passing over his face at whatever thoughts he conjured. "I swear to the gods if Émerin–"

"No!" Renata yelped. "No, gods, Aes, please don't involve him!" *Please don't confirm his suspicions.*

"Then what is it? I don't fucking care if you're the worst Weaver out there or if you can't even touch the First Harmonic at all! I don't care about any of this, Ren, if it means you pretend I don't exist!"

"You are a good man, Aeslev. It's not you, please know this. I have... my family... it's not..." Ren kept pausing, interrupting herself as her thoughts ran wild, fighting against the urge to unfold herself to the person she trusted and the voice screaming at her to run away. *Tainted, bloodied, twisted. A hunter, not a lover. A killer, not a mother. Find the Betrayer, not find love!*

Aeslev slid his hand up to the back of her head, intertwining his fingers with her silken hair. A gasp escaped her trembling lips as his other hand found the small of her back. She looked into his eyes, one black as her shadows and the other a sea of green and gold, trying to discern his thoughts. Surely he couldn't love her, couldn't desire her more than a life among the Named Houses.

"Ren, please don't make me say it."

"Don't say what?" she said, choking on each word.

"I saw you the other night." His voice dropped to a hushed whisper, but the fires in his eyes smoldered brighter.

Renata bit down on her cheek, trying desperately to quell the cry forming in her throat. *I know, oh gods, it was thrilling to know you watched as I moaned your name.*

Aeslev continued, his fingers tracing a swirling pattern across her lower back as he spoke. "I know why you run from me. Why the Songbird no longer spreads her sweet melodies. Why you leave for weeks on end, disappearing into the night like a ghost."

Every part of the woman should have screamed for freedom, should have fought to get away before Aeslev could utter the words on the tip of his tongue. Her entire life had been shrouded in secrecy, living one life under the sun and another under the moon. Never before had the mask slipped, had anyone outside of her family even so much as glimpsed the Shadow-weave she held so dear.

Instead, Renata closed her eyes and let the sorrowful Song of the Night creep into her soulsong. Gods, how she craved to let the man holding her hostage see the truth. How much longer could she fight her heart?

"I knew it," Aeslev breathed.

He leaned forward and brushed his lips against hers, his breath intoxicating her senses. The Shadow-weave tore from her heart, coiling around the woman like a viper ready to strike.

A black umbral cloud cloaked the two. A chill spread over her body, fighting with the heat of Aeslev's palm against her head.

"Ren, you are, gods... you are *beautiful*."

For the rest of her life, Renata could never quite recall her exact thoughts in the moments after Aeslev called her and the dark gift tainting her blood *beautiful*. Something deep inside the woman broke, as if a cord wrapped around her heart was suddenly cut loose. Tears cascaded down her face, sparkling in the soft moonlight like liquid crystals.

Renata wasn't sure if she said anything, or even uttered a sound, before she crushed her lips into Aeslev's. In a singular moment, every doubt and fear she held back from the world faded to oblivion. All she needed was this man in her arms, holding her as if she were the most precious thing the Seven Sisters ever created. His lips moved against hers, the warmth of them pulling her into a blanket of safety. He moaned her name in her mouth, and she could almost taste the desire burning inside the man she'd called a friend since she could talk.

Aeslev pulled away at last, panting for air as a smile broke out across his face that had been solemn since her return to Av Madhira.

"Ren," he whispered. "I need you."

Seven

BOUND BY SHADOWS

AESLEV COULDN'T BE SURE which hurt more: his heart, racing like a wild stallion across the sun-hot sands, or his tongue from biting it four times in the last two minutes alone. The blood ran hot in his quivering arms, muscles unaccustomed to exerting such force against a woman so desperate to leave.

Ren, wait.

Even before he uttered the words, his heart had already made a choice. A terrible, joyous, damning, bliss-filled choice. The shadowy maiden quivering underneath him held the man's heart, not the Daughter of the Sun, with her bronzed auburn hair and sparkling eyes. No, the Lady Naraniél was never his to

39

claim, even if it meant turning his back on a life all of the lower castes would kill to attain.

For years, his heart quickened whenever Renata drew near, when her fingers strayed across his skin a moment too long, or when her eyes lingered when she thought him unaware. Never before did he allow himself to indulge such a fantasy and chase after the woman. Renata made it clear—or so he thought—that she never desired a lover. Not that she felt herself *unworthy* of love.

I will make every day of her life a reminder of how much I love her.

A wide smile broke out across his face at the thought. Renata, forever in his arms; it was all he wanted, not fame or wealth or children with divine blood.

"Ren." Her name came out like a cry for mercy, years of repressed feelings bubbling over inside. "I need you."

Renata did not reply, but her eyes shone bright as the full moon, their silvery gaze bewitching Aeslev. His hand pulled away from her head, tracing the curve of her neck to the low hemline of her dress. The thin black silk gave way to his hungering touch; he slipped his palm under her breast and pulled the dress down with the other.

"Wait," Renata murmured. Aeslev could barely focus enough to comprehend the meaning; Renata stood before him, her naked body glowing with a silvery sheen in the moonlight.

"I—"

"You first," she murmured.

A shade, half-formed in the shape of a man, pulled Aeslev away from the woman. His blood ran cold where the shadows wrapped around his wrists; any thought of fighting back drowned in the waves of desire overwhelming all thought. Renata lunged forward, ripping at the low-cut silk shirt he had received as an engagement present mere hours before. The orange fabric tore with ease—a welcome reprieve from the fires racing across his skin.

"Please, Aes," Renata cried, her voice a strangled sound even as she tore at his clothes. "Please say you don't want me." Her eyes searched his, the shadow behind them growing with each passing moment. "I will be your doom."

"Why would I ever say that?" He fought against the shadows around his wrists, tearing one hand free and wrapping it around her hip and pulling her closer. "I would rather die than live without you."

Her eyes burnt bright, dancing as if he set her soul alight. Her voice—always so calm and measured—quivered with each breath, every emotion on display. It pulled at something deep within Aeslev, urging him to wrap his arms around the maiden and show her that every fear she held was a mere fantasy.

"Aeslev," Renata began to protest. "You don't know what I am."

"And what are you, Renata, besides my closest friend? I've never believed in dark curses and babies that can end the world." He pulled her hand down to his hip; her fingers trembled as they grazed across his bare skin.

"I've never cursed the Dark Goddess nor the Shadows." His mouth found her neck, and he inhaled deeply. *Vanilla.* Gods, the woman always smelled like vanilla.

"And I know that you are the furthest thing from evil, Renata."

A sigh escaped from her quivering lips, the air tickling Aeslev's neck. He softly kissed her under the ear, letting the coolness of her skin ease the desire burning across his mind. Her hands roamed across his bare back, tracing the outline of every scar painting his deep brown skin.

"We should not indulge this fantasy," Renata rasped, but she made no move to get away.

"Why must it be a fantasy?"

"You will be untouchable soon and I—"

Renata's words cut off as Aeslev lowered his mouth to her breast, gently rolling his tongue over her nipple. His teeth grazed against her skin; she shivered underneath his touch. His cock throbbed, hot blood rushing through his veins, searing every cell with one desire: *her*.

"One night, Renata. Please, please give me this one chance. I, oh gods! I will die if you don't let me taste you, please you, love you."

"Why do you want me? Want this?" she whispered while tracing his jawline. He kept staring into her eyes, desperately hoping she would see the answer.

"Why does anyone fall in love, Ren? I could spend a thousand years telling you all the ways I love you, and even then the list would be woefully incomplete. I only know that I love you. Fiercely. Desperately. So much that I would burn everything our masters give us and take a hundred more lashings just to feel your hand in mine one more time."

Despite the cold clinging to the dead winter air, desire for the maiden pressed against his body burnt so hot in his loins that Aeslev could not fathom how he was still alive. The shadows shrank away. He threw both arms around Renata, hoisting her up into the air. Her legs wrapped around his hips, cool skin easing the fires waging a ruthless war with his body. He carried her to the far end of the courtyard and gently set her down on the soft moss at the base of one large golden-yellow tree.

Aeslev moved to kneel beside Renata, but she grabbed him by the shoulders instead, pulling his full weight on top of her. A gasp escaped her mauve lips. He pushed his hips into hers, parting her legs with ease as his hands grabbed the fullness of her ass.

"Aeslev. Please, oh gods, please, I want you."

"You will have all of me, Songbird," he murmured into her ear before nipping at her earlobe. She quivered underneath him. His cock throbbed with need.

"Then this must come off," she rasped, tugging at his loose pants.

Aeslev rolled to the side and pulled his pants off. Renata looked at him with hungry eyes, taking in every inch of the naked man lying next to her. She reached a timid hand out to his cock, then pulled back.

"I... hmm. This seems strange, but I need to confess something. Aes, I, well, I've thought of you. A lot, for a few years now. I get this urge, this burning need and, oh gods, you must think I—"

"I think you love me, and only did what anyone else in love would do. In truth, I've thought of you before. And it was glorious."

Renata looked deep into his eyes, and he could almost see a weight lift from her heart.

"Aes?"

"Yes, Ren?"

"Can I, um, can I touch you?"

A smile broke out across his face as he nodded. He took one of Renata's hands and placed it over his cock, wrapping her fingers around his thickness. He pulled her hand down, then let go. She kept stroking, her hand gripping harder, hungering for more. Her eyes turned black, and a strange look twisted her face.

"All this is mine," she snarled as she lunged forward.

Renata's lips devoured his, teeth scraping against his tongue before hers pushed in. A whimper escaped from Aeslev as a tendril of shadows curled around his neck. She pulled away, her eyes black as the moonless night.

"That celestial bitch will never have you. You've always been mine! I know you watched me in the lake, cried my name as your seed spilled into your hand. Fuck, Aes, do you know how hard it was to not claim you right there?"

"You... you knew?" he choked out, the shadows at his neck dizzying every thought.

"Why do you think I made a noise?"

Renata pushed him back, positioning herself on top with one fluid motion. Aeslev tried to focus on her words, but the heat of her arousal so close to his cock overwhelmed his senses.

"Why do you think I made you watch as I used my fantasies of you to bring myself to bliss?"

One hand pushed against his chest while the other guided his throbbing erection to her entrance. A warmth rushed over him as her wetness brushed against the head of his cock.

"Sisters be damned, Ren," he groaned, pulling on her hips. She fought back, keeping just the tip of his erection against the one place he needed to be.

"If you want me, you have to play by my rules, Aes." Silver streaked across her black eyes, shadows swirling around her, wrapping around her skin until she was wreathed in darkness.

"Anything, Ren."

"Then choose a safe word, and try not to scream too loudly."

Eight

MIDNIGHT PROMISES

R ENATA STUDIED AESLEV, GAZE sweeping across his body nearly vibrating with anticipation. His cock throbbed with each erratic beat of his heart, the swollen head teasing her every time it pushed in just a little further.

Anything, Ren. He would do anything for me, breathe for me, love for me, die for me. Yes, yes, you are mine, oh, why did I ever try to reject you?

"Midnight," Aeslev whispered. "That's my safe word, Ren." He caught one wrist in each hand, pulling them both to his chest. "Do whatever you want, you've always owned my heart. My Songbird, my beautiful girl. Please use me, I want to make you sing again!"

The last vestige of Renata's reservations faded away as Aeslev's words burnt themselves into her mind. Use him, love him, claim him. Yes, she would do it all and never let him go.

Renata closed her eyes and focused on the music thrumming in the back of her mind. She pulled a strand of the song to the forefront of her mind as she formed the weave into a shadowy blade. The cool feeling of metal rested in her palm, and a weight grew as the black blade wove itself into existence.

"Ren?"

"Don't worry, Aes", she purred as she opened her eyes. "I would never use this on you." She set the blade against her left palm; the cold metal pulled a gasp from her throat. "In my family, blood holds power. Not the kind these Maidens of the Sun wield. An older, stronger power. They call our blood tainted, say our dark gift will end the world. If you want me, Aeslev, you must taste what the Betrayer seeks."

Aeslev looked up as if entranced, his different colored eyes both swirling with the other's colors. He rested one hand on her hips, the other tracing the blade's edge.

"You must be a siren, for I'll do anything you ask of me," he said before slicing the tip of his finger.

A droplet of bright crimson blood welled against the black blade before dripping onto Renata's palm. She smiled, then pulled the blade across her hand. A burst of pain leapt from hand to head, burning everything in its path. It faded with her next breath as the Shadow-weave curled around her broken flesh. The blood began to spill forth, dripping onto Aeslev's chest.

"Drink," she commanded as she shoved her bloodied palm against his lips. His tongue pushed against the cut, but the pain was lost amidst the reverie of giving her blood to the man she loved.

"Feel the Song of the Night reweave your soulsong until it beats in time with mine."

She pushed her hips down, savoring the feeling of Aeslev's cock splitting her open, sliding the length of his erection into her wetness. He bucked underneath her, but kept sucking against her palm, taking more of her Shadow-cursed blood in his mouth. She pulled her hand away, then slammed down her weight on his cock. He groaned, eyes fluttering as she took him deep.

"Oh," he whimpered as she sat up, then took his full length again.

"Ren." He thrust into her, his throbbing cock pressing against her clit.

"Use me."

Renata bent forward, her kiss hungering to taste her blood mixed with his saliva. She sucked on his tongue, her hands around his neck as the shadows pulled his hips close. She set a slow pace, luxuriating in the feeling of his thickness stretching her open, pushing against the back of her core until she became untethered.

Aeslev tried to quicken the pace. She stopped, pushing her full weight into him before wrapping her shadows tighter around his throat. Tears clouded his eyes as he gasped for air, but never once did he cry for mercy.

"You will do as you're told," she hissed in his ear. He nodded, eyes wide with a strange look she couldn't decipher.

Renata released his throat, trailing her hands up to his curly black hair. She wrapped one strand around her forefinger before pulling; Aeslev yelped in reply before nuzzling into her hand.

"Would you turn your back on the Named Houses for me?"

He could only nod, bucking his hips up as she squeezed against his cock with her core. A shudder ran through her body, a spring coiling inside her getting stretched more and more with each thrust.

"Would you kill to protect me?"

Aeslev grabbed her by the waist with his broad hands, pulling her up before slamming her down.

"I would kill anyone you wanted, Ren."

A bolt of lightning surged forth from his right hand, sending a shock of energy crackling across Renata's skin. She shivered, her body crying for more.

"Would you worship the Dark Goddess for me?"

She bent over and kissed his neck, pulling the flesh up between her teeth until a whimper filled her ears. She let go, fighting to control the shadows that begged to claim the man beneath her hips.

"I worship you, Songbird."

He pulled her left hand to his mouth, tongue finding the raw cut across her palm. He teased the sensitive flesh, pain mixing with the pleasure building inside until Renata could barely remember to breathe. Aeslev's hand at her hips kept pushing her back and forth, his hips rocking her clit against his cock. He stopped every few seconds, letting his throbbing erection pulsate in her core.

"That's it, that's my girl," he crooned as he pulled her hand away and placed it over his heart. "Come for me, Ren. I want to feel your ecstasy on my cock."

The closer to the edge Renata got, the harder it became to command the shadows. Aeslev's words snapped the last of her resolve; the black Shadow-weave surged forth, wrapping around Aeslev's body, sinking into his flesh and pulling a strangled scream from his throat. His eyes rolled into the back of his head, the whites now black as night. He bucked and thrashed under her hips. She grabbed his hands and pulled them to her ass, helping guide her along his length.

Renata could feel the end, taste the release that she had dreamed of for six years. The crescendo built, sweeter-tasting than it ever had been before.

"Yes, oh gods, fucking yes! Take me, take it, ta—"

A wave of pleasure crashed over Renata, drowning her senses in an earth-shattering ecstasy that felt like every orgasm she'd ever experienced at once. She could barely comprehend the feeling of her core pulsating around Aeslev's cock. He lay still, eyes now closed, shadows still curling over his body. His hands trembled against her hips, the only sign he was still alive. Renata collapsed against his chest, desperately trying to suck in air through her parched mouth.

The two lay tangled in each other's arms for some time, the gentle fading throbs of Aeslev's erection competing with the waves of bliss still lapping over Renata's exhausted body. The shadows withdrew as she slowly came to her senses. She rolled off to the side, but the hands of her friend-turned-lover never strayed from her skin.

"Ren," he whispered after some time.

"You never said midnight," she said back, her voice soft.

"Did you expect me to?"

"Did my shadows hurt you, Aes?"

"It was a good hurt. I've never felt so alive." He leaned forward and kissed her, his lips soft against hers. "I've never felt more at home."

"And my blood?"

"It set mine on fire." He pulled her forehead to his, a deep sigh filling the air.

It couldn't be true, but here he was anyway. The man Renata fantasized about since her eighteenth nameday, when she woke up one day and realized she didn't just love Aeslev, she *loved* Aeslev. She silently thanked the Dark Goddess for sending him to the lake the other night, for making him stay as they pleasured themselves while thinking of the other. Forbidden lovers, using each other in the dark to chase a fantasy they both denied themselves.

But it would not stay a fantasy forever.

"Aes?"

"Yes, Ren?"

"Will you marry me?"

Nine

A GIFT

WILL YOU MARRY ME?

How was Aeslev supposed to focus on anything else when the words he'd always wanted to hear finally spilled from those delicious, perfect, succulent lips? His mother prattled on about the wedding preparations, seemingly oblivious to the fact that her son had just violated his bonds before they could even be made.

"And what of that orange silk shirt Émerin gave you? I think the color complements your eyes so nicely, the Lady Naraniél will surely agree. We should get another made for your ceremony, but with our House symbol on the hemline."

Aeslev shot out of his chair, unable to continue pretending nothing had changed less than six hours ago. He licked his lips—the iron from Renata's blood still lingering on his flesh—before placing a hand on his mother's shoulder.

"Mother, please stop."

"What, do you think you know better? Oh, silly me, Naran—"

"MOTHER!" he yelled, thunder echoing around him as he spoke. "That is enough. I am not marrying Naraniél."

Aeslev's father jerked his head around, beads at the end of his braids slapping against each other. "What did you just say? Tell me I misheard, son."

Son. He never used Aeslev's name when he was upset. So predictable, just like the lightning that streaked across the room toward the young man. He ducked, sending a shot back to his father, aiming just above his head.

"Try it again, *Father.* I'm done playing your fucking games. You do not scare me like you once did."

"Aeslev!" his mother cried. She tried to stand up, but his hand clamped down, shoving her back in her seat.

"No, gods! Just listen to me for once! Both of you!" He paced the wide kitchen where they had gathered for morning breakfast, stormclouds trailing behind him.

The Skyweave lurched inside, tearing at his mind as he tried to contain his rage. Years of hatred for his parents built with each passing moment, all the times he did what they wanted for House Caledir instead of following his happiness. He groaned at the thought of making Renata wait so long; they could have been married for years now, building a life together far away from the watchful eyes of their masters.

"Did it ever occur to either of you that I care more about my happiness than the future standing of our House? I was happy, fucking elated when Nessaeren said that sniveling little shit was her *liraes.* I don't know what she sees in the man, but gods, I didn't care as long as it meant I was free from being sold off like livestock. I don't want to join the Named Houses, I want Renata. I've always wanted her, and I don't care that she barely has enough power to be called a Sunweaver. She... she's different, special."

His mother could only utter, "Sold off?" while his father simply shook with anger. Too late; Aeslev continued, unable to stop now that he opened his heart.

"Sometimes, I don't know if you love me, or if you love the idea of me. I wish I weren't so powerful; I wish I could be ordinary, free to love and marry who I want. I don't want Naraniél, or any other woman from beyond the Wall. I want, no, I *need* Renata. I don't care if that makes me a failure in your eyes, if you want to pretend I am dead or never existed. She loves me, loves me just as I love her. How could you not want that for me?"

His mother stood, her dark brown eyes thick with tears. She reached a hand toward Aeslev before dropping it at her side.

"Son," she whispered. "Aeslev, my baby. Of course I want you to be happy!"

"Phyrra," his father growled.

She waved her hands at him dismissively.

"Go away if you have nothing kind to say. Now."

There was a fierceness to her words Aeslev had never heard from his mother before. His frantic heart calmed ever so slightly as he realized she wanted to protect him. His father stalked off, muttering under his breath as thunder followed his footsteps.

"Ignore him, Aes. Look at me, my sweet boy. Please."

She gathered his face in her hands, fingers tracing a gentle swirling pattern across his temples. He relaxed into her arms as a sob rumbled forth from his chest. He couldn't remember the last time his mother held him this way. The last time she comforted the man trying to make sense of a world ruled by divine descendants of the lost Sun Goddess, everyone vying to prove their worth—and thus, secure their future. Love was something afforded to very few; what did Aeslev do differently than anyone else to deserve such fortune?

"I love you, I love you so much! That's why I've pursued this marriage for you. I thought that's what you wanted. You've always talked of the great men from our House who joined the Named Houses. I thought... well, I thought wrong, it seems." His mother's lip quivered as she spoke, her tears threatening to burst forth.

"Mama," he choked out. "Mama, don't cry, please."

"How can I not? I've failed you! I only ever wanted you to be happy, oh Aeslev, how could I have misjudged your desires so badly?"

She pulled him into a hug, squeezing before letting him go again. He wiped the stray tears from her face, caressing the wrinkles on her warm brown forehead. *You'll look like the clays after we bring rain,* he used to say as a child when she first lamented over the signs of age. She smiled as if she too recalled the memory.

"It wasn't just your fault; I denied it myself for too long as well. I thought Ren could never love me, so every time I had to choose between her and our House, I told myself my feelings didn't matter. How can I be so stupid?"

"Love makes fools of us all, Aes. You know I love your father, even when he angers me. The Sisters know our marriage isn't perfect, but that doesn't mean it isn't worth the effort and heartache. If you love her, chase after her! Do not marry just to satisfy your parents."

Aeslev studied his mother's eyes, looking for some sign that this was all an elaborate trick. But he found nothing except love and compassion in her gaze, and with each passing beat of his heart, he came to accept she truly valued his happiness above all else. She brushed a stray curl behind his ear, cupping his cheek in her hand as a small bolt of lightning raced across his skin. The tingle spread through his face, calming his restless mind.

"I miss you doing that, Mama," he whispered. "Why did you stop?"

"I don't know, baby. I think I thought you didn't want me around. I love you, you know that, right? Just tell me what to do, and I'll help."

He thought for a moment, pondering how to secure his marriage to Renata without alerting the *Makhaeren* and potentially exposing his lover's secrets. He needed a plan fast.

"Do you trust anyone at the Temple, Mama?"

She pursed her lips for a moment before breaking into a smile. "I know the perfect woman. She is my closest friend from the Academy. I know she will help if we ask. Does this mean you intend to marry Renata in secret?"

"It's the only way I can think of keeping her safe. If the *Makhaeren* finds out I denied Naraniél just to marry a weak Sunweaver... I know they say soulbonds are sacred, but Ánnarsera killed that woman last year. Oh, gods, Mama, if anything happens to Ren, I swear, I'll, I'll, I'll kill everyone here!"

Lightning raced across his skin, the sound of thunder rumbling behind his words. The thought of losing Renata tangled with the Skyweave until he was sure he would unleash a storm where he stood. The touch of his mother's fingers on his forehead helped cool the anger rising inside.

"I will not let anything happen to either of you, Aes. I promise this with my life. If Renata is worth it to you, then she is worth it to me. I will always support your happiness, your future, and your choices. My parents let me choose your father, and it was the greatest gift they ever gave me. I only want to do the same for you. My only son, my sweet boy!"

"I love you, Mama," he sobbed.

"I love you, too, Aeslev. Now, we have a wedding to plan!"

Ten

POSSESSION

I'M GOING TO MARRY *Aeslev. I'm going to be his wife, his soulbound, his lover. Gods, can it be true?*

Renata paced the long corridor of the Temple, thumb circling one of the golden hoops dangling from her right ear. She could almost feel the sandstone beneath her feet wearing away with each step. *How long does it take to learn my next assignment? Sisters, help me!*

"Weaver Renata." A woman's clear, sharp voice rang out from the entryway at the far end of the corridor. "Come."

Renata spun on her heels, gaze landing on a tall woman dressed in bright white silks. Her crimson-red hair fell in tight coils to the floor, hundreds of gold bands stylized like flaming suns wrapped around each one. Deep amber eyes surveyed the young woman. A frown pulled at the corner of her mouth.

"*Makhaeren* Ánnarsera," Renata said, dropping to her knees as she spoke. *Goddess help me, why is she here?* She kept her head bowed, not daring to gaze too long at the woman blessed by the Sun Goddess herself.

"Rise, *neha*. Follow, quickly now."

The High Priestess of the Madhiri and the first daughter of the first daughter for generations past of the Sun Goddess, the woman in white seemed to burn as hot as the sun itself. Renata always felt her shadows buck and shy away in her presence. She drew in a breath to steady her nerves, then stood and walked forward. Ánnarsera tapped her foot with each step; Renata quickened her pace.

Soon enough, she entered a brightly lit courtyard, tall grasses and lilies of every color imaginable lining a small paved circle. Towering above it all at the far end stood a tree with golden-yellow bark. Beneath it, she knew, was a bed of moss crushed by the insatiable appetite of two lovers the night before. A smile spread across Renata's lips at the memory, but the clicking of the *Makhaeren's* shoes chased it away. Ánnarsera strode across the circle, then sat in a simple wicker chair and beckoned for Renata to kneel.

"Do you know why you are here, *neha*?" she asked as Renata sat. The divine woman's eyes seemed to burn through her; she felt a scream building in her throat as the Shadow-weave recoiled.

"To receive my next assignment, *Makhaeren*."

The less Renata showed her fear, the better. Somehow, she had the feeling the woman lording above her could tell she violated Aeslev with her tainted blood. Why else would the High Priestess herself come and speak to a lowly Weaver with few useful talents?

"It's come to my ear that the masters of the Hénar winery you were sent to last year found your performance less than satisfactory. Even High Lord Émerin noted your inability to maintain sunny conditions for a mere week when he was stationed there. Why do you think that is, Renata?"

That fucking snake! I'm going to kill him, I swear to the Seven I will!

Renata gulped down the cold winter air, then stared into the *Makhaeren's* eyes, trying to discern what trap the woman had set for her.

"I believe the task was too much for one Sunweav–"

"Yet Émerin's Sunweaver was able to finish the job for you."

"But we worked together!" Renata protested, anger flaring despite the icy hatred in the *Makhaeren's* eyes.

Ánnarsera stood and walked forward until she loomed over Renata, bright silks nearly blinding the woman cowering below. Renata dug her fingernails into her hips, trying to distract the Shadow-weave crying out in her mind. *Run, run, run before she kills you!*

"Weaver Renata, I will say this only once."

The *Makhaeren* bent low, brushing her lips against Renata's ear. Her blood began to boil inside. A sweat broke out across her skin until she thought she might burst into flames.

"Unless your next assignment in Apathren comes with glowing reviews, your status as a Weaver is forfeit. You will be stripped of all rank and titles, and sent to live in the Slums where you and the rest of the Unblessed belong. Do I make myself clear?"

Renata could only utter a half-formed "yes" before collapsing on all fours. She sucked in short breaths, her body refusing to work as her mind spun out of control, unable to focus long enough to form a thought. The taste of bile crept into her mouth, followed a moment later by the remnants of her breakfast. She coughed and spluttered as hot tears ran down her face.

It seemed as if hours passed before Renata choked back the tears and sat up. Ánnarsera was nowhere to be found, the woman alone in the courtyard where, not even twelve hours ago, she thought she had finally found happiness. *How naive can I be? Why did I ever trust that fucking backstabber to help? I should have known he would use it against me!*

As if summoned by her thoughts, Émerin strode into the courtyard, a knowing smile on his face. Renata tried to look away, but his muddy brown eyes clawed at her, demanding her attention.

"Kneeling, just how I like my pretty girl."

He stood next to her now, his fingers running through Renata's hair. She flinched under his touch, but could only shake with anger. One wrong move and her shadows would burst forth, and then a fate worse than death would find her.

"Tell me, Sweet Renna, what did our illustrious leader say to make you so compliant? A feisty thing like yourself must have been cowed, indeed."

"Why won't you let me go, Émerin?" she sobbed.

"You awaken something in me that no one else does. You feel it too, don't you? The way our soulsongs pull at each other."

"You have a *liraes*, and it's not me." Renata tried to sound fierce, but her words came out as squeaks.

"Oh, not a fated lover, Sweet Renna. Something older, more primal." He pulled her head back, forcing her to look into his eyes, now pitch black. "Something darker."

"I am nothing like you," she whispered.

"Oh, Sweet Renna. You are very much like me. One life under the sun, another under the moon. You remember those nights we etched our names into the other's flesh."

"You will never have me, Émerin," she said through clenched teeth, fighting to hold back the shadows threatening to swallow her whole. "Never!"

"Did you know your eyes turn silver when your cum covers my cock? You're already mine. I will have you again, one way or another, Renata. Only you can calm this storm inside my mind."

Something inside Renata snapped. She twisted around as she called forth a strand of the Shadow-weave, just enough to wrap around Émerin's wrist and pull it from her head. His fingers tangled with her hair, ripping a chunk from her scalp as his hand jerked back. Renata sprang to her feet, chest heaving as she struggled to keep her shadows in check. Her vision darkened until she could only see a dark shade where Émerin stood. *Do it for him, come on, Ren!* The thought of Aeslev's arms around her quelled the shadows enough; the song faded out until it rested once more.

Émerin stumbled back, his eyes wide as a strange black cloud gathered at his feet. Then, before Renata could blink, it disappeared.

"You... you... you're..." he stammered, clutching his wrist to his chest.

"Say it, Émerin," Renata snarled. "It takes one to know one, doesn't it? That's why you've chased me all these years, why your family teeters on the edge of oblivion. Tell me, did you always have a black heart, or did it die with your parents?"

"You fucking CUNT!" Émerin screamed as a bright light blinded Renata. His fingers scratched at her wrist, but she recoiled in time.

"I will have you, Renna, and then I'll shut that pretty little mouth of yours for good."

Renata kicked her foot out, catching her assailant in the stomach. He groaned as he fell backward, hitting the garden pavers with a loud *CRACK*! Shadows swam across Renata's vision; she ground her teeth, forcing the Shadow-weave back inside.

"Do you really want to tell Ánnarsera about my shadows? What will happen when she asks for proof, and you can only say, 'trust me'? Nessaeren may have inked her family's doves on your hands, but you will never be a part of their world."

Émerin stood, chest heaving as a trickle of blood ran from his left ear.

"It would be worth it to hear your screams as she burns both of us to death." He lumbered forward a few paces before falling to the ground. "Why didn't you love me, Renna? What does he have that I don't?"

Suddenly, Émerin looked so pathetic, his once-clean robes now dusty and smeared with blood, a look of heartbreak in his usually cruel eyes. Renata backed away, the exit from the courtyard only a quick dash away.

"He is a better lover than you in every way imaginable, Émerin. You wanted to possess me. He wants to set me free. You will never be even half the man Aeslev is. I pity Nessaeren, truly. For her sake, I hope you never have a daughter. And if you do, I hope she sets fire to your world."

Émerin tried to stand, but a black shade clawed at his heels, dragging him back down. A pathetic whimper escaped his throat. Renata couldn't help but laugh at the sight before her: a High Lord, reduced to a beggar while the woman who rejected him chased the one she truly loved. If no other blessings came to her in life, Renata knew she would die happy.

"Fuck you, Émerin. Crawl back to your wife. I have never been yours."

Renata turned and walked away, letting her shadows hold the man down until she was well clear of the garden. She broke into a run, not stopping until she stood on her doorstep.

Eleven

FREEDOM IS ALWAYS EARNED

"WHERE IS HE?"

The words flew from Renata's mouth before Aeslev's mother had a chance to open the front door more than a crack. The young woman shoved past her, eyes wild as she scanned the room.

"Where is Aes?" Renata sucked in a breath through her teeth, trying to calm the shadows seething inside. "The shift leader said he was dismissed early today."

"Renata, how lovely to see you!" Phyrra exclaimed, rushing forward to stop Renata from tearing the front room apart. "He's not here. What's wrong?"

"There's a…" Renata trailed off, unsure how much to reveal. "A complication that I need his help with."

Renata eyed the older woman, marveling at how young she still looked despite her abundance of wrinkles. A light shone in her eyes that had not been there before. *Does she… did Aes tell her?* Renata took Phyrra's hand in hers.

"Phyrra," Renata began, but before she could continue, the older woman pulled her into a tight embrace.

"Renata, my child," Phyrra murmured. "We have it all taken care of. He's meeting with a *Makhiri* we trust right now."

A small weight lifted from Renata's heart at the words of her future bonded mother. She smiled, then sank into Phyrra's arms.

"Oh, Phyrra, it's not just that!" she sobbed, the rush of emotions from confronting Émerin finally taking their toll. Her stomach flipped as salty tears poured from her eyes, stinging her cracked lips as they fell to the floor.

"That snake, that *shain'sa* snake won't let me go! He has a celestial wife, and still, he wants to own me! He, he, he will tell the *Makhaeren* if I don't comply, he'd rather see me dead than not with him! I can't marry Aes, I can't bring this doom to him!"

Phyrra's wrinkled hands wiped the tears from Renata's face, the warmth of her touch easing the chaos inside. She cooed a lullaby of sweet nothings in Renata's ear and held her until the sobs began to fade.

"No, shh, don't say such things, Renata. My son loves you, all of you! He told me Émerin tried to hurt you last night, but it won't happen again. You may not know this, Renata, but he will do anything asked of him by that woman who so unfortunately found herself fated to his bed. Nessaeren is a strange woman. She may not control her husband's heart, but she can control his actions."

"How do you know this?" Renata asked as she untangled her arms from Phyrra's embrace.

"Why do Dreamweavers know anything? All it takes is a simple message, and Émerin is as tame as a chained dog."

"It was you, wasn't it?" Renata gasped. "You sent that woman in green to take him back!"

A coy smile flitted across Phyrra's lips before disappearing.

"Or perhaps the High Lady Nessaeren found her bed empty, and her desires growing. Whatever may be the case, I hear the messenger arrived when they were needed most."

"Oh, Phyrra! You have always been so good to me. I don't know what I've done to deserve such happiness."

"You are a unique woman, Ren–"

A deafening crack of thunder drowned out Phyrra's words. Renata ducked on instinct. The thunder rumbled again, closer this time. The air practically crackled with energy; the hairs on Renata's arms stood up as shivers crawled across her skin.

The front door flew open. Aeslev rushed in. His chest heaved as lightning raced across his skin, both eyes nearly black with rage. They softened the moment his gaze settled on Renata; the darkness withdrew, and his eyes that she fell in love with, one green and one dark brown, grew wet with tears.

"Ren," he choked out before hoisting her in the air.

She threw her arms around him and buried her face in his neck. Shocks of energy tickled at her skin, the Skyweave still out of his control.

"Ren, Émerin told me you, oh gods, I can't say it!" He kissed her, devouring her until she could barely breathe. "Songbird, my Songbird, I'll never let you go again!"

"I'm never going anywhere," she whispered back.

Aeslev set her down on the ground, his hand never leaving the back of her head. Phyrra walked up and placed a hand on his shoulder.

"Don't worry, Aes, I have a plan. Stay here and keep Renata safe. I have a High Lady to visit." Phyrra leaned up and placed a gentle kiss on her son's cheek. She turned and retreated into the back of the house, disappearing behind a curtain of beads.

In her absence, Renata could only focus on the taste of Aeslev on her lips and his hands still trembling against her bare skin. She leaned her head against his chest, letting the rhythmic rise and fall quell the fear fighting to take hold of her heart.

"When he said you willingly went with him behind the Wall... Seven help me, Ren, I thought I might destroy the oasis right there."

"How could you believe him?" Renata shoved Aeslev away. "Believe I would do that to you?" she asked, shocked he could think so lowly of her.

"No! I thought he abducted you! The only reason he is still alive is because I was sure I'd never see you again if I killed him!"

Aeslev shook with anger, stormclouds gathering at his fingertips. "I will still kill him, Renata!"

"You can't!" she shot back. "Please, Aes! Think about what you're saying! He is a High Lord now, you know he is untouchable. We just... we just need to run away. We'll wed tonight, say our goodbyes, then tomorrow wake up far away from this place. We can go back to Isneha, I'm sure the Academy would employ you as a master Skyweaver!"

"I won't let him dictate our lives, Ren!"

"What about what I want?"

Aeslev paused; the stormclouds disappeared as he sighed. "What do you want, Renata?"

She took a step forward, then placed one hand over Aeslev's heart.

"I want to be happy. With you, Aes. And I don't care where we live, or what we eat, so long as you're with me. You say leaving would mean he wins. I say it means we can live freely."

"So we leave, just like that?"

"We can return if you want, but please give me this chance."

"What if he follows you?"

"He has a wife who owns his fate. He will never stray far from her."

Aeslev chewed the corner of his lip, deep in thought as he stroked Renata's dark auburn hair. She took his hand in hers, interlacing their fingers together.

"Are you certain this is what you want? A life with me, and another man always in the back of your mind?"

"You give him too much power, Aes. I chose you, and I'm sorry I didn't all those years ago. It was always you, ever since we were children, it was you. You're my best friend, and the only person I ever want my thoughts to linger on. I love you, Aes."

Aeslev bent his neck forward and kissed Renata, a soft and gentle kiss that caressed the fullness of her lips, then swept down to her neck, a dozen little kisses trailing in a row. The breath hitched in her throat as his lips passed below her collarbone and across her upper breast before pulling away.

"You are my world, Renata."

Renata smiled, her heartbeat quickening at his words. Whatever hardships would come their way, Renata knew nothing could tear them apart. Not a scorned lover, the High Priestess, or even the gods themselves. She would kill for Aeslev, kill anyone who dared try to take him away. She would be his protector, and she, in turn, would give herself fully to the man who knew the shadows tainted her blood and still wished to make her smile.

"After tonight, I will be yours forever, Aeslev."

THE DARKEST NIGHT

THE SIGHT OF RENATA dressed in pale blue silks, the soft fabric hugging her curves and drawing out her ethereal gray eyes, forever remained the most beautiful vision of Aeslev's life. Even as his lover grew older, her figure fuller, and her smile brighter, the sight of his bride under the soft midnight moonlight was the closest thing to divinity he saw in his long years. Her long auburn waves fell to her waist. A silver tree with white gems surrounded by a crescent moon hung from a thin chain, nestled between her breasts and the low neckline of her dress.

Though direct descendants of the Sun Goddess, the women of the Houses of the Sun could never compare in beauty to the woman before him. Renata, the one who held his heart: a Goddess, if he didn't know better.

They stood hand in hand on the edge of Lake Anataerl, the cool water lapping at their bare feet. A woman with short brown hair twisted into knots stood behind them tying a white ribbon over their clasped hands. Aeslev only knew her as the *Makhiri* his mother said they could trust. He paid her little mind, his eyes trained on Renata and her unearthly beauty.

I love you, she mouthed, her eyes sparkling silver in the pale light.

I adore you, he mouthed back.

The priestess in white finished tying the last knot in the ribbon. Her hands fell away; before she could prompt Aeslev, he began to recite the handfasting vows.

"Your hand in mine, my hand in yours. *Maí feilira.*"

"Always I will find you, and you will find me, *maí feilira,*" Renata said back.

"We bind our hands, for you are pulled to me, and I to you."

"My hand in yours," Renata continued. "Your hand in mine, bound under the sun and moon."

"May the road rise to greet your feet, and the wind be always at your back." The priestess spoke with a soft voice as she placed a single thread of gold silk over their hands. "Let the sun's warmth shine upon your faces and the cool embrace of the moon guide you home. May the smile never fall from your lips, words of loss and sorrow never heard upon your tongue."

Aeslev looked deep into Renata's eyes, now almost pure silver. She looked happier than she ever had, even more than the night they finally gave in to desires that burnt for years. A single tear fell from her eye; he reached out with his free hand and wiped it away. She nuzzled into his hand, closing her eyes as a soft sigh escaped those perfect lips.

"This is the hand that will wipe the tears from your eyes, be it sorrow or joy, and each time I vow to bring a smile back to your face."

He spoke with an earnest desire that burnt through his heart, setting the man aflame. He needed Renata to be happy, *needed* to see her incandescent smile again and again until it never faded from her face.

"And this is the hand that will hold you in the darkest hours of night," she whispered back, placing her free hand over his still against her cheek. "When fear and grief fills your mind, I vow to bring a smile back to your face."

"I reach for you, and you reach for me, even across the Endless Void," they said in unison.

With their final words, the gold thread was tied around their bound hands. Tears ran down Aeslev's face, overcome with emotions he could only barely describe. Elation, unfettered desire, a bliss greater than anything he'd felt before.

"Under the Light of the Seven Sisters," the priestess said in a hushed voice, "be at peace. Know each other as your *feilira*, as soulbound lovers, blessed by the Sisters themselves."

Aeslev kissed Renata as their onlookers—the priestess and both their parents—let out cries of joy. He moved to pull his wife in closer when a shout wrenched his attention away. Panic set in, heart racing as he lifted his gaze in time to see a flaming orb streaking across the lakeshore aimed at Renata.

"REN!" he screamed as he threw her aside.

They collapsed on the sandy shore of the lake. She scrambled to stand up, choking as she moved away from where they stood.

"Kill her, kill her now!" A woman's sharp voice pierced the night sky, malice dripping from every word. Aeslev blinked, eyes focusing on the *Makhaeren* Ánnarsera. "Do not touch Aeslev!"

"Oh, Sweet Renna!" Émerin taunted. "Look what happens when you deny me, Sweet Renna!" His cruel laughter filled the air as another flaming orb hurtled toward them.

Aeslev pulled himself upright, trying to protect Renata from the fireballs the *Makhaeren* threw at her. The Skyweave inside seemed to respond on its own; a thick cloud of fog formed at his feet, thunder rolling overhead as lightning struck the ground next to Émerin. The man leapt to the side with ease, eyes flashing as if he thought this a game.

"Aes, over here!"

In his panic, he lost track of the priestess and their guests. He jerked his head to the side to see his mother and Renata's father helping his new wife scramble away from another fireball. Wisps of shadows gathered at her feet, but they retreated as a blinding light filled the sky.

Aeslev tried to move, but his feet would not comply. He looked back to see a bright chain, almost as if made of sunlight, wrapped around his ankle. Émerin stood just in front of him, eyebrows knit together in concentration. Aeslev tried to lunge forward to no avail.

"I've got you now, you fucking obstinate little pest," he hissed. "You've had enough fun with my toy." Émerin's eyes looked black as night; a shiver ran down Aeslev's spine at the sight.

"She is no one's toy," Aeslev roared, clawing at the air in front of him. He tried to focus on the Skyweave, but the music was lost amidst the din of the battle around him.

While Aeslev held Émerin's attention, his mother desperately tried to fend off Ánnarsera's attacks. The fog cloud burnt away with the heat of the High Priestess's fireballs. Renata's parents both looked on, too terrified to use the Shadow-weave and expose their family secret. They scrambled away from a fireball; it separated the group, Renata now standing by herself in the direct path of the *Makhaeren*.

"Reni!"

"Renata, over here!"

"RENATA!"

Before Aeslev could react, a blood-curdling scream filled the night sky. One moment, he stared at Renata, helpless as Émerin held him hostage with the Sunweave. The next, a bright orange pyre burst to life where his lover stood, a shadow writhing in the flames as Renata's screams tore through the night.

Émerin burst into laughter, a cruel sound that forever seared itself into Aeslev's mind. The Sunweave around his ankle faltered for but a moment. He rushed forth, tackling Émerin to the ground. He could barely see his fists pummeling Émerin's face through the tears burning his eyes.

"I. Will. Kill. You!" he screamed, each word punctuated by a wild punch somewhere on Émerin's body.

"*AAAAEEEEESSSSSS!*"

Renata's dying scream broke through his cloud of rage. Aeslev looked up, panting as blood dripped from his knuckles. He pushed himself up, looking around for the *Makhaeren*. She stood in front of Renata's burning body, arms raised high as flames leapt from her hands.

She's going to die, she's going to die, she's going to die, die, die, die, die!

The rage fueling his attack on Émerin left, replaced with a sense of utter hopelessness. There was nothing he could do now; even if he managed to subdue the woman with the power of the sun in her hands, Renata would burn until nothing remained but ash and bone. Aeslev crawled forward, sobs wracking his body. Maybe he could touch her one last time, maybe the Sunweave would burn him alive too, and they could die in each other's arms.

"NO!" A man's scream interrupted his thoughts.

Aeslev blinked, and when he opened his eyes, he saw his father lying on top of the *Makhaeren*, fighting to hold her wrists to the sand. Renata's parents and his mother were nowhere to be found.

"Save her!" Aeslev's father yelled.

Aeslev ran to Renata. She lay on her side, barely recognizable under the burns covering her body. Shadows wrapped around her burnt form, a thick cloak of black that almost looked like her skin.

"Ren," he whispered.

She could only whimper in reply.

"Ren, can I touch you?"

She nodded.

Aeslev reached out, gently touching her shoulder. She cried, but did not jerk away from his touch. Her skin was hotter than the burning sands of summer. He gritted his teeth, then pulled her up into his arms.

"Ren, I have you."

She mumbled something incomprehensible.

"Ren, I'm going to save you," Aeslev said, voice quivering with each word. "I promise."

Thirteen

THE MAIDEN OF LIGHT

"REN, I HAVE YOU."

"Hold me, Aes," she tried to reply, but the words stuck in her throat, mixing with the taste of ash and blood.

"Ren, I'm going to save you. I promise."

Renata remembered nothing else after the words said in vain by her lover. Her husband, even if only for a moment. Renata didn't want to die, gods, not when she finally had Aeslev, but at least she would die knowing he gave his heart to her.

Death was never something Renata particularly feared. Where others fell to old age and disease, her family lingered on; perhaps the cursed shadows tainting their blood came with a few beneficial side effects. Whatever the case, Renata always knew she'd live a long life, albeit one without love. Was this the price of chasing what she was never meant to have? As Renata's last thoughts faded to oblivion, she knew the answer: yes.

Yes, if the price of love meant an early death at the hands of the High Priestess, she would chase it every time. Renata smiled—or at least, tried to—then drifted away in Aeslev's arms.

Mama, why do you love Da?

Why do I love you, Little Cub?

Because you made me?

Well, I suppose that's part of it. But I didn't make the Moon, and I love it. I didn't make your father, and I love him.

Oh. Is it because I look like Da?

That certainly helps. But no, that's not why.

There isn't one reason, is there?

Not really, Little Cub. I know that your smile is one of my favorite things in the world. I know that you smell like paradise. I know that your father and I waited so many years to see your face, and when you came, there were two of you! I know that your brother reminds me how lucky I am to be alive. I know that I'd do anything to make sure you find someone to share your life with, too.

Is that what love is, Mama? Knowing things?

It's complicated, Little Cub. Love is a lot of things. Love exists despite Death, despite hatred and foul actions, despite people who want to ruin the world for their gain. But I can't tell you exactly what love is. You just know what it's not. Someone once told me they loved me, but their actions hurt me. That wasn't love, but I didn't know it at the time.

So, how did you learn?

Your father saw me. He saw my shadows, our shadows that fill our blood, and he called them beautiful. He lets me be happy, even if he doesn't understand it all the time.

Do you think I'll ever love someone, Mama?

I know you'll find love, my sweet boy. And when you do, I think you'll change the world, Therat.

"Aeslev, hold her hand right here against my chest. Don't let it move. Renata, can you hear me?"

A woman's soft voice, so delicate it seemed as if the voice of a Goddess, broke through the strange reverie. Something touched Renata's hand. She tried to blink, but her sight remained black. She sucked in a breath, and a wave of pain assaulted her every sense. The air across her burnt skin set her mind ablaze, every part of her body screaming as it tried to process the burns and melted flesh of her desecrated form.

"Renata, just relax, I'm going to make it all go away."

A whimper escaped her throat. She tried to relax and focus on the coolness around her wrist.

"I'm right here, Ren, you're going to make it, I promise, I promise." The pain eased with Aeslev's words. His grip around her wrist tightened.

"Mmmmake me sm-smile ag... again," she forced out, reciting part of their vows they exchanged less than an hour ago.

Aeslev laughed, a bittersweet sound. "Yes, yes! I'll make you smile again, my wife, my Ren, my Songbird!"

Renata focused on Aeslev's words, replaying them over and over as the strange woman recited something in the Elder Tongue. The pain eased over time, though Renata could not be sure how long she lay there. As her senses slowly returned, she opened her eyes. Aeslev's face loomed large in her vision, his green and brown eyes intently studying her face.

"Aes," she whispered.

He placed a finger on her lips; his touch sent a dizzying wave of desire through her.

"Shhh. Save your energy. Nessaeren is almost done."

Renata turned to the side, suddenly aware of the impossibly beautiful woman sitting beside her, eyes glowing green as her whispers filled the air. Renata had never seen the new High Lady of House Isht'iri and the fated lover of the man who tried to kill her. Everything about the woman enraptured Renata; the blue doves and flaming suns tattooed across her hands and forearms perfectly complemented the tight curls of deep red hair cascading down her back. Her round face and full lips looked so different from the Weavers, almost glowing as if the sun lit her ocher-brown skin.

As she gazed at the beauty of the High Lady, Renata noticed a warmth spreading from her hand against Nessaeren's chest. It chased away the lingering pain until Renata felt more alive than ever before. Each beat of her heart pushed the feeling through her body until she felt whole again. Renata slowly sat up, leaning against Aeslev's chest as she gathered her strength. Nessaeren still clutched Renata's hand close to her chest.

"There you are," the ethereal woman said. The green glow dimmed, and sandy brown eyes gazed back at Renata. "Your soulsong was so weak, I could barely find it again. Oh, Renata!"

The woman born with the blood of the Sun Goddess lurched forward and gathered Renata into her arms. Renata froze, unsure of what to do. It was forbidden to touch anyone from the Named Houses; all those in the lower castes knew this well. Yet, Nessaeren used her talents to save the life of a woman the *Makhaeren* deemed an infidel. If the High Lady cared about decorum, she would have easily let Renata die so her sister could marry Aeslev.

"Why are you helping me?" Renata mumbled at last, still tangled in Nessaeren's arms while Aeslev's hands lingered around her hips.

"Your life matters, Renata."

Nessaeren pulled away, a smile on her achingly beautiful face. She tucked a lock of hair behind Renata's ear, her touch softer than water.

"I know you don't think it does. I know you think you are less than me. I might share Myrniar's celestial blood, and you might be the weakest Weaver in the Madhira, but that doesn't mean you deserve to die just because my husband cannot let go of a childhood fantasy. Émerin..." Nessaeren paused, a pained look crossing her face. "He is a difficult man to love."

"I never meant to cause issues, my lady," Renata whispered.

"You did nothing wrong, Renata. In truth, I envy you and Aeslev. Having a *liraes* does not guarantee you love. The gods fated us together for our future child, not because we share love. I knew this when I married him."

Renata sucked in a breath, trying to clear her head of the thoughts swirling inside.

"You don't blame me?"

"I blame the darkness in my husband's mind. I blame him, but never you. I will make sure he never touches you again, Renata. I promise."

Nessaeren took Renata's hands in hers. She traced the length of each finger, a small burst of Sunweave following in her wake. Unlike Émerin's Sunweave, this only tickled her skin and didn't send her shadows screaming into the darkest corners of her mind. Renata closed her eyes, focusing on Aeslev's breath against her neck as the divine woman continued caressing her hands.

"Long ago, my mother taught me the warding bond Myrniar used on her daughter." Nessaeren spoke as she continued tracing Renata's fingers. "The women in my family pass it down to each young daughter to use as we see fit. Most use it to keep their children safe from strangers, but sometimes it is used to protect them from a single person. Émerin will never be able to touch you again so long as I am alive, Renata. He will look at you and see a stranger, hear your voice, and only hear whispers instead. You will disappear from his life, no matter how hard he searches for you. I cannot change his heart, for it was dark long before I knew him, but I can hide you from his cruelty."

"My lady," Renata breathed, unable to say anything else.

"There is no need to thank me, Renata. I have a feeling that one day, people will remember your name. Rest now, please. *Oirith ithé athnea, venaem ithé lira. Cinn buil á anais.*"

With her final words, the High Lady Nessaeren stood, brushing the sands from her green silk dress. Her eyes sparkled as she smiled at the young lovers wrapped in each other's arms, then turned and disappeared into the dark night.

Renata looked around, studying her surroundings for the first time. They sat in an overgrown section of palm and acacias, the mirror-like surface of the still lake stretching out before them. The moonlight filtered in from above, bathing the world below in soft shadows.

The Song of the Night thrummed in the background, and Renata felt truly at peace for the first time in her life.

She turned to gaze into Aeslev's eyes. His hands pulled at her waist, dragging her close until she could feel the beating of his heart against her chest. She crushed her lips into his, trying to taste every part of her lifelong friend who loved her, wed her, and then helped save her life. She owed everything to the man with his arms around her. She needed to feel him against her, inside her, touching every part of her until her skin memorized the feeling of his body against hers.

"Ren," Aeslev protested as her hands pulled at his shirt. "You need to rest, you almost *died!*"

"That's exactly why I need you," she panted. "Show me why I don't want to die."

"You're, you're..."

"I'm yours, Aes."

He growled something, perhaps "yes", then tore his shirt off. He ripped at the shreds of Renata's burnt dress, barely covering anything now. He pulled the fabric away, her skin almost sparkling in the moonlight. He cupped her breasts in each hand as he kissed her, his lips trailing down her neck, her collarbone, between her breasts. She pushed her hips into his growing erection, urging him on. He threw his head back, eyes wild with desire.

"Midnight," he whispered as he pressed his lips against her ear. "My safe word is midnight." Her legs twitched at his words as the need for release built. "Time to make you sing, my little Songbird."

TO MAKE A SONGBIRD SING

T HE SMILE ON RENATA'S face quelled the worries still gnawing at Aeslev's heart. Her silver eyes gleamed like the young moon above as she tangled her fingers through his black curls.

"You saved my life," she whispered, placing one hand over her heart.

Aeslev melted into her soft skin, wishing he never had to let her go. She pushed her hips closer; his cock strained against his pants. His lover—no, his *wife*—sent a dizzying wave of desire through his body, intertwining with bone and sinew until every part of him screamed for her soft touch. He needed her lips against his, around his cock, over his stomach, down his back... needed her sweet words in his ear, her taste in his mouth.

"You are my world, Renata. The air in my lungs, the blood in my veins, the keeper of my soul. I would die without you, Ren."

He moved both hands to her hips, sparks of lightning flying across her cool brown skin. Her eyes swirled with shadows at his touch. She pushed him back, pulling herself up until she straddled his hips. Aeslev could feel her wetness through his thin cotton pants. Before he could move his hands to pull them off, a thick rope of shadows bound itself around his wrists.

Renata leaned over, pressing her lips against his ear.

"That's not what I want," she whispered.

She moved Aeslev's hands to grip her ass. He squeezed, the firmness of her flesh eventually giving way to his hunger. His cock throbbed with each squeeze, and she, in turn, pressed her weight into him a little more each time. Aeslev kept rocking her back and forth, fanning the fires burning inside.

"What do you want, Songbird?" Aeslev stopped moving, waiting for his wife to tell him what to do.

"I want you to make me come with your mouth." The shadows around his wrist tightened, then yanked his arms over his head. "I want to hold you down and force every part of you to show me how good it feels to be alive."

Aeslev groaned at her words, the thought of tasting Renata burning inside since he first fantasized about her. She pulled herself up, grazing her breasts over his mouth as she moved. He sucked on one nipple, teeth nipping at the tender flesh as it passed by.

"Fuck, Ren, every part of you tastes divine," he choked out between the waves of desire washing over him.

"You haven't even gotten to the best part," she laughed.

"Then come here, please!"

Aeslev fought with all his might against the shadows binding his wrists above his head, but they would not release him. A whimper filled the air as he thought of wrapping his arms around Renata's hips and pulling...

"Fight all you want," Renata said with a mocking voice. "It won't help."

Her hips rested against his chest now. He could almost taste her wetness.

"Gods," he breathed. "Why are you torturing me? Let me fuck you, please! Taste you, bring you to climax, whatever you want except pretending you don't exist!"

"You are so beautiful when you beg, Aes."

Renata looked down at him, looming tall as she pressed her inner thigh to his mouth. He pulled the soft flesh into his mouth, kissing her until she pulled away. His tongue flicked out, the taste of salt and something he could only describe as sweet greeted his taste buds. Renata quivered under his touch.

"Goddess help me," she whispered. "How do you do this to me?"

Aeslev stretched his neck forward, lips brushing against the softness of Renata's core. She groaned as his tongue licked her skin, hot with the same desire burning inside Aeslev. She sank into his devouring touch until he took all of her in his mouth. Spasms of ecstasy rushed through his veins as Renata shook above him, pressing herself a little more against his mouth each time.

"Fuuuck," she managed to say at last between moans. "Oh, Aes, how, how…"

"How what?" he asked, words muffled as he kept flicking his tongue over her flesh, teasing her entrance but never giving her more.

"How," she panted, breath ragged as he grazed his teeth over her clit. Her thighs squeezed against his head, the pressure amplifying the blood rushing past his ears.

"How do you know what to do?" she managed to choke out.

Aeslev pulled his head back, looking up to meet Renata's gaze.

"How do I know how to breathe? I just know I want to make you scream my name until even the Seven know that I am the one you chose."

Shadows filled Renata's gaze; her eyes turned black as night. She tangled her fingers through Aeslev's hair, then pushed his mouth back between her legs. The Shadow-weave binding his wrists tightened, and the cool feeling of shadows spread. They looped themselves over his arms and around his neck, squeezing until he fought for each breath of air.

Aeslev's mouth never moved, every thought bent toward bringing Renata to completion until she was a quivering mess of flesh and bliss over him. He swirled his tongue over her clit and nipped at the tender flesh. A half-uttered scream tore from Renata's throat, her back arching as she hummed with pleasure.

"Yes, oh gods yes, Aes," she moaned. "Don't stop!"

She pulled on his hair harder, pain mixing with the pleasure swimming in his veins. Aeslev kept swirling his tongue over her clit, pushing it against her entrance before pulling back and grazing his teeth over the hot flesh. Every movement sent a jolt through Renata's body; the more she squeezed, the faster his tongue moved. His hips bucked up, the spasms leading to his eventual climax near impossible to control.

"Oh, *fuck*, Ren," he groaned through the shadows at his neck. "Fuck, I'm going, oh I'm going to—"

Before he could finish his thought, an unearthly chill settled over his body before sinking in. The air evaporated in his lungs as shadows swam through his veins. Unlike before—when he didn't know what to expect—Aeslev let them take control. He closed his eyes, ready to let the Shadow-weave claim him.

Through his building bliss, Aeslev kept teasing Renata's tender clit; she tried to move away from him, but the shadows around his neck wrapped around her hips, pulling her back down. He silently thanked them, then quickened his pace as his tongue pushed against her entrance.

Then, before he had a chance to prepare, an explosion of pleasure burst across his mind. He shoved his tongue inside Renata as his cum shot forth, seed spilling on his stomach. He tried to push past the blanket of bliss surrounding him, to no avail.

"Yes, yes, oh gods, Aes, I love you!"

Steeped in the throes of his orgasm, Aeslev barely registered Renata squirming above him, squeezing her thighs until she collapsed on all fours. He pulled her in close, pressing his lips against her stomach as she rolled to the side.

"Never leave me, Ren," he whispered at last. "I need you."

DEAR WIFE

R ENATA SIGHED AS IMAGES of the previous night flashed by.

Aeslev, dressed in black and gold, his eyes shining under the glow of the silver moon. His lips against hers, their hands bound together as husband and wife. A fireball landing at her feet, and an agony so great her memory could not process the pain. The Shadow-weave screaming as the Sunweave burnt her from the inside. An impossibly beautiful woman with scarlet hair, her smile as brilliant as the Sun.

Nothing could have prepared her for the first hours of her secret marriage to Aeslev. Was this an omen of what was to come? A sign from the universe and the Seven that chasing after his love was a mistake?

Renata shook her head, trying to clear the thoughts haunting her. *He loves me, he saved me. It does not matter what anyone else says.* But even as she tried to convince herself of the words, a nagging thought in the back of her told her the *Makhaeren* would never let her live. Émerin may never look at her again and see the woman he wanted to claim, but Lady Nessaeren's talents surely would not save her twice. Renata shuddered, unsure what to do, then looked around the Temple courtyard.

A headless statue of Myrniar stood in the center, surrounded by a veritable thicket of brightly colored wildflowers. The Goddess held the sun with both hands, raising it high above where her head would have once been. Renata studied it, wondering what the Goddess would say about one of her Daughters saving the life of someone tainted by the dark. It still didn't seem real that Nessaeren would somehow find them and help heal the woman set on fire by the leader of the Madhiri. Why Nessaeren risked everything—including her station as High Lady—was beyond Renata.

Renata's stomach lurched as a young woman wearing a simple white dress beckoned for her. She stood at the far end of the courtyard. Though it was not a long walk, Renata relished every second, secretly wishing she could somehow stop time and never have to face the *Makhaeren*. She tried to remember the promise

Nessaeren made, and the letter she sent requesting the young lovers come to the Temple to set things right. But Renata could still feel the Sunweave turning her body to ash; the fear nearly buckled her knees as she walked.

All too soon, Renata reached the young woman in white. She did not say a word, simply nodded her head, and began walking. Renata followed her, too scared to think of anything except her breath. *In, in, in, out, out, out, out.* After what seemed like minutes of endless twists and turns, they finally came to an open atrium. A leafless tree with golden bark towered above the courtyard below, its massive trunk shading the world from the harsh afternoon sun.

The *Makhaeren* sat atop a simple dais, the Lady Nessaeren at her side. Aeslev already knelt before them; he stirred as Renata entered, but did not lift his gaze to greet her. A shiver ran down her spine; was he already subservient, forced to bend to the *Makhaeren's* will? Was... was she going to force him to marry the Lady Naraniél?

A scream tried to wrench free from Renata's throat at the thought, but she clamped her mouth shut. She would *not* show the woman any fear.

"Kneel, Weaver Renata."

"*Makhaeren* Ánnarsera," she replied as she knelt, averting her eyes from the woman's gaze.

"It seems I owe you an... apology."

Ánnarsera paused as she spoke, as if loath the utter the word. Renata wondered if she had ever said it before.

"My niece has explained the actions of her husband, and the history between you two that he did not think relevant to share when he accused you of *unnatural* waveweaving skills. This does not excuse a secret marriage, but you do not deserve death for this mistake."

The words of the woman who, less than twelve hours ago, tried to kill her did little to assuage Renata's fears. Though Lady Nessaeren's smile beamed down on her, Renata knew this could only be an elaborate ruse meant to trick her into saying the wrong thing. Surely Ánnarsera of all people would never admit to making a mistake.

"Let it be known, Weaver Renata, that while I do not approve of my niece's protection of you, even I do not have the power to undo Myrniar's Blessing. Use it well, *neha*, for you are the first outside of our blessed Houses to receive such protection. If it were not for her actions, you would be dead and Aeslev soulbound to the Lady Naraniél. If her choice to save your life ever brings harm to the Madhira, I will make the Dark Goddess herself delivers both your soulsongs to the Endless Void."

Renata kept her head down, smiling under her hair at the *Makhaeren's* veiled threat. *If you only knew how much I desire to see Her.*

"Yes, *Makhaeren* Ánnarsera," she said, trying to placate the woman who still saw her life as a mistake. "I thank you and Lady Nessaeren for your blessings. I will always work to ensure the prosperity of our great home."

Ánnarsera stood, looming large over Renata and Aeslev, still kneeling before her. A scowl crossed her face before she walked away. Nessaeren lingered, stooping low to level her gaze with Renata's.

"You will bring greatness to our home, Renata. I feel it in my soul. Go now, be at peace with your love. I am sorry for everything you have endured thus far. I will make sure Ánnarsera keeps her word. Myrniar's Blessing is a bond even she would never think of breaking."

"My lady," Renata said, unsure how to thank the divine woman for saving her life now twice over.

"You do not need to thank me. I only did what anyone would do for love. *Póch'ir u'la, Renata'iri. Eásiri fei na seraí, mi tou itu' shoi.*"

With her final words, the High Lady Nessaeren of House Isht'iri, with her scarlet hair and soft brown eyes that danced in the sun, turned and walked away, disappearing into the dark corridors of the Temple. In her absence, the world seemed a little dimmer, and the birdsong not nearly as sweet.

Though Renata would never again see the High Lady, for the rest of her life, she dreamt of the celestial woman. Though she cursed Émerin to never father a child, in her heart Renata hoped the gods would send a daughter their way, a woman with a heart as kind as her mother's and as fierce as her father's. A woman to change the world, to lift the hatred seeping into the souls of the weary Children of Eás.

"Ren."

Aeslev pulled her into his arms, dragging her into his lap. He stroked her hair with one hand, the other tracing the outline of her lips. His eyes, one dark brown, the other a brilliant emerald green, swept across her face, studying her as if looking for something.

"Ren, we made it. I don't know how, but we did."

"We owe everything to Nessaeren," she murmured. "She saved me, protected me, petitioned for me. I... I don't know why. I'm nothing special."

Aeslev's mouth twitched. "You are my wife! That makes you special to me."

"And to her?"

"Perhaps she sees something neither of us can. The Daughters of Myrniar know more secrets than they share. Maybe she thought you deserve happiness, or maybe there is something greater than both of us that is yet to come."

Renata nuzzled further into Aeslev's arms. She thought back to the future she once dreamed they would share, before she convinced herself she was not good enough for the man who had always loved her. The places she wanted to show him, from the Silver Forest to the Ever-night Mountains, watching the rising sun from Aemyn Cet and the setting sun over the Andesiri River. Wherever she was, Aeslev would never stray far from her side. The thought put a bright smile on her face.

"What makes you smile so?" Aeslev asked as he placed a kiss on her forehead.

"Our future."

"And what is in our future, dear Wife?"

"Sights you cannot imagine until they are seen, strange music, and even stranger people. My family lives across the world, our shadows hiding us even amongst those who seek to kill us simply for breathing. I want you to meet them, Aes. I know I must seem ashamed of this dark gift in our blood, and some days, I was. But you've shown me that I don't need to live two half-lives. I can live under the sun and the moon as one, so long as I have you."

"That is all I ever want for you, Ren. To be happy. Utterly, completely happy. To smile every day from sunup until sundown, and to smile even brighter under the moon. To love me, hold me, walk through life with me hand in hand. I will never leave you, Ren. Even if I have to die to stay with you, I will. Forever."

"Oh, Aes!" Renata cried, overcome by the depth of her love for her husband. "Aes, I will be here as long as you want me!"

"I'll never stop wanting you, Ren."

Renata turned to the side, catching Aeslev's mouth in hers. She kissed him deeply, desperately trying to show how much she needed him.

"I want it to be just the two of us for a long time, Aes. But I do want a family, one day."

A name came to her, a name she heard in that strange reverie when she thought she would die. A vision of the future, perhaps? At the very least, a vision of the future she wanted.

"I want a son, and his name will be Therat."

Aeslev cupped her cheeks, pulling her forehead to his before kissing her again.

"One day, then, Ren, we will have a son named Therat."

In the back of her mind, nearly lost amidst the sorrow of the Song of the Night, a hushed woman's voice whispered in reply.

That is a good name, a strong name. A name that will change the world.

ABOUT THE AUTHOR

D. KATHLEEN GREW UP in the foothills of the Willamette Valley watching the sun rise over Mt. Jefferson each morning.

An only child, from a young age, D. Kathleen always felt more at home with her nose in a book, preferably something with magic, mythical beasts, and a badass female protagonist. Combined with far too many times watching movies like Beauty and the Beast, Labyrinth, and Bram Stoker's Dracula, it was always a foregone conclusion that she would end up falling for the morally gray villain.

As an author, D. Kathleen combines her love of high fantasy, dark romance, and mental health awareness. She currently resides in Southwest Washington with her husband, two cats, and a plethora of wild birds demanding offerings. When not working, writing, or reading, she can be found outside in her gardens, marveling at the beauty of nature.

Also By

Daughter of the Dark Sun: Songs of the Night Volume One
Dove of the Blood Moon: Songs of the Night Volume Two

SCAN BELOW FOR SHOP